SR

D1388914

The Devil's Gold

Dennis Rumble wasn't a good man but he wasn't entirely bad. He had principles, after all. He wasn't anything like the notorious band of outlaws calling themselves the Coyotes, into whose territory he was obliged to travel.

He was a man with a mission, determined to rescue a beautiful woman snatched from the stage by the outlaws. As Rumble was soon to learn, though, things are not always as they seem. Twists and turns lay ahead of him and many men, some more deserving than others, were destined to lose their lives over what Rumble called 'The Devil's Gold.'

The Devil's Gold

M. Duggan

A Black Horse Western

ROBERT HALE · LONDON

© M. Duggan 2010
First published in Great Britain 2010

ISBN 978-0-7090-8882-0

Robert Hale Limited
Clerkenwell House
Clerkenwell Green
London EC1R 0HT

www.halebooks.com

Typeset by
Derek Doyle & Associates, Shaw Heath
Printed and bound in Great Britain by
CPI Antony Rowe, Chippenham and Eastbourne

CHAPTER

'Say the word and you are out of here!' Judge Thompson looked down his long nose at the piece of garbage seated on the opposite side of the warden's desk.

Dennis Rumble's expression did not change. The silence between the two men lengthened.

'Answer me damn you!' the judge yelled. He could not curb his annoyance. Anyone other than Dennis Rumble would have jumped to accept his offer of a pardon and cash.

'What ain't you telling me, Judge?' Rumble queried mildly. 'Spit it out,' he encouraged. 'I know you are holding back. I smell a stink and I want to know what's causing it.'

'Nonsense,' the judge blustered. 'I've made you a generous offer. All you have to do is fetch my daughter home. I'm offering you a small fortune and a pardon.'

'Spit it out,' Rumble reiterated. 'Or I'm headed back to my flea-infested cell.' Unexpectedly, he smiled. 'I'm not a fool. I'm your last port of call. I know you, Thompson. You wouldn't spit on me if I were on fire. You wanted to hang me for murdering Sam Grey. But Grey's pa twisted your arm and got me a life sentence. He wanted me to suffer!' Rumble paused, he watched the judge. 'Old man Grey is dead, ain't he! He ain't around to cause a rumpus if I walk free! How'd he die? I'd like to know!'

'He was struck by a runaway horse and carriage,' the judge snapped, 'An unfortunate accident which robbed the city of a good man.'

Rumble nodded. He'd bet that it was no accident that had robbed the city of a good man, but now was not the time to challenge the judge.

'You worthless bum!' the judge couldn't help himself. 'We both know you're a no-account assassin. Men have died because of you!'

'We both know I didn't kill Sam Grey,' Rumble replied. 'I was framed.'

'You've sent plenty of men to meet their Maker,' the judge countered. 'I know about you, Dennis Rumble. From an early age you've been associated with a house of ill-repute. And those patrons who upset the proprietor, well, they risked meeting an early demise. That woman paid you to do them in. And after her there were others. How many women have paid you to murder their men! You're garbage, Rumble!'

'You know that I am the only man likely to succeed in rescuing Miss Lilly from the owl hoots holding her. That's why you are here.'

'You are correct,' the judge retorted coldly.

'How did you learn about my skills, Judge? I am curious to know.'

'That's not your concern!' the judge look a deep breath.

'What's your answer? I haven't got all day.' It was time to call the felon's bluff.

'You've sent others after Miss Lilly,' Rumble stated flatly. 'And they've failed. I need to know what happened to my predecessors. I need to know what I'm facing. What kind of men am I dealing with?'

'Scum like yourself,' the judge rejoined before he could stop himself.

'That's as maybe. But I'd still like to know what happened to my predecessors.' Rumble winked. 'It's time for you to spill the beans. I'll know if you keep anything back. I'll know if you lie. I can always smell a liar. You do right by me and I'll do right by you. You will see your daughter again. Now let's hear what you've been keeping from me.'

The judge hesitated. He had no choice. The ruthless killer seated opposite stood a good chance of bringing Lilly home, No one else would touch the job now. They were too damned scared. 'There have been two others before you,' he grudgingly admitted. 'The first was basted with fat and roasted over a low fire. And the second was skinned alive!' Rumble's expresaion, he saw, did not change. 'So do we have a deal?'

'Yep. We have a deal,' the assassin replied.

'I anticipated your compliance. I'll have the pardon signed and you'll be freed with all possible speed.'

Rumble smiled, but the smile did not touch his eyes. 'I need to learn all I can about the galoots who have your girl. I reckon the newspaper office is a good place to start. Groundwork, Judge! That's what it's all about.'

'You're not afraid?' the judge essayed.

'I understand men who enjoy killing and inflicting pain,' Rumble replied carefully, before concluding. 'But I am not one of them.'

'You haven't answered my question.'

Rumble sighed. 'Only a liar never admits to fear. But I have belief in myself. I've always achieved what I set out to do. I do not contemplate failure. I will fetch Miss Lilly home if she still lives. You have my money ready when I'm set free!'

'What's to prevent him taking the pardon and running for his life?' demanded Warden Godwin, a short, fleshy individual, eyes lost in rolls of fat.

'Yeah. What is to prevent me?' Rumble enquired.

'You'll bring my girl back or die in the attempt,' the judge replied with certainty. 'I've found out plenty about you, Dennis Rumble. You ain't quite alone in the world, are you? I believe you have a sibling, a respectable—'

'That's enough. Button your lip or I'll knock your teeth down your throat.' Rumble's face suffused with rage.

'Excellent. I've found your Achilles' heel. Now I know you will do your damnedest to succeed. How will you set about getting my Lilly back?' Judge Thompson asked as if Rumble's outburst had not occurred.

'I have no plan as such,' Rumble replied. 'Other than to say I guess my predecessors aimed to snatch Lilly and get out of the territory pretty damn quick. That won't be my way. It should be as clear as the nose on your face, judge, that to ensure our safety I'll have to dispose of the whole darn bunch of them.' He shrugged. 'I see no other way. I am a conscientious man, so rest assured I'll do my darnedest.' He paused. 'Very likely your daughter has

gone loco if she's thrown in her lot with these cut-throats!'
Or the girl was smarter than she'd been given credit for.

'Just fetch her home, Rumble, fetch her home,' the
judge rejoined. 'It's true, Lilly must have lost her senses or
she would not have run away from a loving home. The
female mind is not strong, Rumble. And when it breaks no
fault can be attached to the unfortunate female. Bring my
Lilly home. I'll make you a rich man.'

'I'll bring her home.' Rumble rose to his feet. 'If any
man can fetch her home I am that man. Now I'll bid you
good day.'

'Dennis Rumble is a conceited varmint!' Warden Godwin
declared once Rumble was on his way back to his cell. 'I
hope you know what you are doing, Judge Thompson,
setting a mad dog like him free.'

'Regrettably I need him,' the judge replied. 'You keep
him safe for me, Warden Godwin. If anything happens to
Dennis Rumble I'll destroy you. Rumble is my only hope.
It is imperative I get my daughter back.'

'When you get her home I'd advise you to dispose of
him. He's liable to bite the hand that fed him,' Godwin
stated sourly.

'You sound afraid, Warden Godwin. Do you imagine
that one day Dennis Rumble may decide to come after
you?' The judge chuckled. 'Rest assured I have plans for
Rumble. I entirely agree that mad dogs need to be
disposed of.'

Dennis Rumble lay in his fetid cell. He had plenty to
think about. He knew the judge to be a devious varmint.
He needed answers to a few questions before he headed

west to rescue the judge's runaway daughter. According to the judge the girl had headed west in search of adventure. The stage on which she'd been travelling had been held up and the owl hoots had killed the men and taken Lilly. Later there'd been reports of a woman who could have been Lilly riding with the murderous band.

Judge Thompson was waiting when Ramble, now a pardoned man, came through the gates of the penetentiary. The judge held out an envelope. 'As agreed, a third now, the rest payable when Lilly is safely home.'

Rumble took the envelope. 'Anything you want to say before I get on with the job?'

The judge smiled unpleasantly. 'Now we're alone let's put the cards on the table!'

Rumble nodded. 'You ain't disappointing me, Judge. You're living up to my expectations.'

'If you fail me, Rumble, your former landlady is going to meet with an accident. She will be meeting her Maker sooner than she might wish. Do you understand me?'

Rumble nodded. 'Perfectly.'

'It was hard to find the chink in your armour, Rumble, but you lodged with that woman for quite a while before you appeared in my court. I believe you might therefore have some concern for her continued good health.' He waited, but Rumble remained silent. This irked the judge. He wanted to hear the man bluster and issue futile warnings, but Rumble merely nodded. 'And of course there is that other matter . . .' he continued.

Rumble shook his head. 'Now I *am* disappointed in you, Judge Thompson.' Then, without waiting for a response, the ex-felon turned on his heels and strolled away. Before he headed west he aimed to set Judge Thompson straight. And he'd be able to settle a score at the same time. But right now he was headed for the newspaper office. He really did need to learn all he could about the outlaw band who had taken Lillian Thompson, the judge's only child.

By the time he'd finished ploughing through back issues of the goddamn paper his eyes ached. He rubbed them with the backs of his hands. He'd read so many back issues of the city's most popular paper that he'd lost count. The boring repetition had been worthwhile. He'd pinpointed the area where the polecats were holed up. The men he sought were in close proximity, he believed, to a frontier town named Upstanding.

The room where the back issues were housed was filled with dust. Motes danced in the sunlight gleaming in through a dirty window. As he rose to leave he became aware that he was not alone. He recognized the man who had just entered the room. Presumably to plough through old papers, just as Rumble had done.

'You ain't worth a spit, Rumble,' the other stated without preamble. 'You're a goddamn coward who has always lurked in shadows. When men are counted you won't be among them.'

For a moment he thought Captain Epson, the bounty hunter, would block his path.

Epson laughed. 'Quit shaking in your boots. I ain't interested you, Dennis Rumble. Like I said, you ain't worth a spit.'

Ignoring the man Rumble left the room. Epson was a man who only went after the money. There was no reward on Rumble's head so right now Epson was not a threat. He stood on the pavement outside the newspaper offices. He was ready to head west. He was ready to go after Miss Lilly but first he needed to know things about the woman, things he wouldn't get from the judge. And of course there was the matter of the errand that most be attended to.

He was annoyed with himself. He'd grown soft. He had never imagined that anyone would seek to frame him, Dennis Rumble, respected member of the community. Epson had been correct when he had spoken of shadows. Rumble had not revealed his true self. And yet Judge Thompson had learned how it was that Dennis Rumble, orphaned at an early age, had done so well for himself until of course he'd been framed for a killing he had not committed.

Dismissing his past with a shrug, he returned his thoughts to Miss Lilly. What he wanted to know about her he wouldn't get from the judge. He decided he needed to speak with Miss Lilly's old governess. This presented a problem, as Thompson had seen to it that the woman had been committed to Weedington's Private Asylum. She'd been committed about ten years ago: round about the time Miss Lillian Thompson shut herself away in the house. Or had been shut away by the judge.

Colin Weedington listened patiently as the man explained what he wanted. The man was quietly spoken. Weedington did not anticipate trouble.

'What you ask is quite impossible,' he explained patiently. 'I cannot release a lunatic into your care even if,

12

as you claim, you are related to her. Miss Clegg's been certified as insane. Judge Thompson's own physician signed the certificate. She's being well cared for here.' He shook his head. 'I cannot allow you to distress her further.'

'I thought that's what you would say.' Moving with a quickness that startled Weedington, the man came to his fret. Too late, Weedinston realized the walking-cane concealed a sword, the tip of which was now pressed against his bulging stomach.

'This will slide in like going into butter,' Rumble observed cheerfully. 'I suggest you reconsider. What do you say?'

Weedington nodded vigorously. His bulging stomach rumbled. 'Judge Thompson!' he stuttered.

'Need never know. He's not likely to enquire about her and if he does you'll think of some excuse.' Rumble was somewhat surprised that Miss Kathleen Clegg, one time governess to Miss Lilly, was still alive: an oversight on the part of the judge, he was sure. 'Now take me to her.' He exerted just enough pressure to cause a drop of blood to stain Weedington's shirt. Weedington squealed like a hog!

'I'll take you to her. You can take her away,' Weedington babbled.

Rumble sheathed the sword. 'I knew you were a reasonable man. Let's go get her.'

'You'll wish you left her here. She won't be the same. She's been here too long!'

'Quit gabbing. Lead the way.'

As Weeedington led the way from his office his legs felt as though they had turned to jelly; he could scarcely walk, so great was his fear.

13

When Rumble set eyes on Miss Kathleen Clegg he cursed. Weedington's private asylum had not treated her kindly.

'I'm here to set you free, Miss Clegg.' For a moment he thought she was going to attack him. 'I ain't no friend to Judge Thompson,' he clarified.

She nodded. Her expression became sly. 'If you want me to answer your questions you must first do something for me. Unlock the doors, Mr Whoever you are. Otherwise you must haul me out of here fighting you every step of the way.'

'That doesn't seem a sensible thing to do, ma'am.'

'But I'm mad. Or I would not be here. Doctor Weedington will vouch for it that I am mad. Give me the keys!'

'Hell. Why not!'

'And keep Doctor Weedington by your side.' Her eyes glinted dangerously.

Weedington shuddered. It was night. Prospective clients, he had found, preferred to visit at night. His staff slept. At night the place was unattended, save for the half-witted night watchman. Keepers were only called in at night when a new inmate was scheduled for arrival, for, naturally, new inmates were always troublesome before it was knocked out of of them.

Rumble took Weedington's arm and propelled the man along in the wake of Miss Kathleen Clegg, who seemed well-acquainted with the fetid, dimly lit stone corridors of the asylum. As heavy doors swung open she called out.

'They'll be rounded up. This is pointless,' Weedington wheezed, but Rumble ignored him. His stomach heaved at the sights emerging from locked cells.

'Are we done, ma'am?' he croaked, wanting to get out of this hell-hole pretty damn quick.

'It's done!' She laughed hysterically. 'And so is Weedington.'

From both ends of the corridors women lurched towards Weedington.

'Here he is!' Kathleen Clegg gave Weedington a shove. With a howl he overbalanced.

Women pushed past Rumble and pounced on Weedington, tearing at him with long filthy nails. There was nothing Rumble could do even if he had a mind, for others howling madly rushed to join in.

And Rumble was very much afraid that once they had finished with Weedington they might turn on him. Gripping Kathleen Clegg's thin arm he steered her out through the back door and then through the back gates of the asylum. There was no sign of the watchman, which was just as well because he might have been obliged to kill him.

'Most of them will be found and locked up again. You know that.' He propelled Miss Clegg into the carriage he had waiting.

'But perhaps one might make it.' She sighed.

'I aim to see you safely out of the city, Miss Clegg,' he reassured her. 'Never doubt you'll be beyond the reach of Judge Thompson.' With that he set the horses in motion.

Judge Thompson poured a brandy. He'd sent his man Mullin to try and determine what had taken place at Weedington's asylum. Instinct told him Rumble was involved. But he could not ask Rumble. It would be unwise to show concern. For all the judge knew Clegg might have died. Thinking back, he recalled that Weedington had been instructed to detain the woman but not to finish her off. Indeed, the judge had soon forgotten about the troublesome governess, the woman who knew too much. Since then he'd had no dealings with Weedington other than to recommend him to men who had troublesome women they wanted put away.

A piercing scream broke the silence. More screams followed. It sounded to the judge as though every female servant in his house was screaming. He lit a cigar, then, clamping it between his teeth, he made his way slowly downstairs.

A large leather bag had been left on his doorstep. Staring up from the bag was the severed head of Mullin, the man who'd framed Dennis Rumble for murder. Find a scapegoat, the judge had ordered, never imagining that his man would choose Rumble, a complete stranger to both of them. Only much later, when the judge had been looking for a killer to deal with the vermin who held Lilly had Rumble's nefarious past come to light.

And there, standing across the road, arms nonchalantly folded, was Rumble himself. At ease, he sauntered across the street and confronted the judge. 'Anyone you know?' he enquired.

'What's your point?' The judge didn't waste words.

'I don't much care to be framed for a murder I did not commit, although I know I was selected by chance. It was nothing personal, after all!' Rumble paused before continuing: 'Why I do believe this was the man ready and waiting to occasion harm to my one-time landlady?'

'No man is irreplaceable,' the judge smiled.

'I know that. But word is out now: any man who even thinks to cause me grief, well that man is liable to lose his bead. It ain't a question of feelings, Judge, it's a question of respect. I can't be threatened with impunity. I don't give a damn that you had Sam Grey killed, and maybe old man Grey, but when a drunken fool starts to proclaim loudly that Dennis Rumble is running scared, scared of what's going to happen to a lady he used to lodge with, well, let's say I felt obliged to reply in a way galoots of a certain kind will understand.'

'You've heard, then, what happened at Weedington's?' Judge Thompson dispensed with caution. 'Weedington was unrecognizable. He was practically torn to pieces. They used their teeth. And then they set fire to his office. Records were destroyed.'

Rumble shrugged. ''Just one of the risks, I'd say, when a man makes his money running a private asylum. Now have you anything to say before I head west in search of Miss Lilly?'

'As far as the world is concerned my daughter is safely at home with me.'

'Yep. You kept her shut away until she got out.'

'My daughter suffers from a delicate constitution. As far as the world is concerned she never went west. She was never taken by owl hoots. That's all you need to know.'

'I believe Captain Epson will be heading west.' Ramble paused. 'The railroad has brought him in. He is at this moment negotiating his fee. Captain Epson, unlike many in his profession, is an honest killer. He won't spare her because she is your daughter.'

'I believe you are quite capable of dealing with Captain Epson should it be necessary. I'll try and delay his departure to afford you more time. Naturally there's always a chance that it will be Epson's head that ends up on a post and not the owl hoots responsible for the atrocities out west.' The judge sighed. 'I regret the fact that Epson is honest. I would have preferred you to rot in the penitentiary. But we understand one another. As for Mullins, if he were so lax as to allow you an opportunity to cause harm he's not worth a spit, as Epson would say. Now I am going to put my cards onto table. You will fetch my daughter back because you know very well that mud sticks and anyone connected with you, even if they are unaware that they are connected with you, why, that person would never be able to wash way the mud.' The judge paused. 'I'm certainly not threatening you. I am merely telling you how it will be.'

Rumble smiled. The smile did not touch his eyes. 'Rest assured, Judge Thompson, your daughter is coming home.'

CHAPTER 2

His journey west was uneventful. As the train didn't go as far as Upstanding a large part of the journey had to be done by stage. Still trying to figure out the best way to get the girl away from the owl boot band he climbed aboard the Upstanding-bound stage.

After he had spoken with Kathleen Clegg he had visited a certain orphanage. From what he had learnt he knew that Miss Lilly had been headed for a town called Poynton when the stage had been waylaid and she had been taken. From his reading of the back issues of the newspaper he'd realized that there was a circle around Upstanding where the gang did not raid. Poynton itself was just within that circle. Miss Lilly had just been outside of the circle when the stage had been held up.

Somewhere in that circle, very likely near to Upstanding, the murderous bunch had to be holed up. The terrain around Upstanding was mountainous, according to a map he'd studied. He was a city man unaccustomed to the West and he acknowledged this put him at a disadvantage.

'In you get, missy.' The stage door opened and a short fat woman clambered in. Carefully she settled herself in the furthest corner. He'd seen her once before in better times. He had also seen her on the train coming west. She watched him with ill-concealed disgust. Realization was slow to dawn. As he eyed her coldly it came to him with a feeling of annoyance that she had to be following him.

'What brings you West, Miz Broughton?' he asked without preamble.

Harriet Broughton boiled with righteous indignation. 'What brings you West, Mr Rumble. I am sure my leaders would like to know!'

'Your pa may own the paper, Miz Broughton. But the only readers you have are fool women who like to read you describing the fashion in bonnets. Who was seen wearing what! I've read your articles. I ain't impressed!'

'I know how you paid for your schooling,' she hissed. 'I know how low you sank.'

'It was your pa who told Thompson of my speciality!' She blanched but did not respond with a denial. 'And the only way you could know anything about me would be if you'd had your ear to the goddamn keyhole!' He paused. 'Your damn fool of a pa pays folk to snitch. And someone snitched about me.'

Harriet Broughton was terrified he was going to grab her and try to force the information from her. She remembered the day she'd taken the carriage and had ordered their coachman to drive her to a certain establishment of ill repute. Eventually a woman had emerged from the house, a huge creature practically bursting out of her red velvet gown. She'd heaved herself into a waiting carriage and driven away. She had been Miss Clara, the woman who'd sent work Dennis Rumble's way.

As the stage jolted along Rumble figured things out. He came to the conclusion that Miss Clara had deliberately sent the snitch to old man Broughton. She was a cunning woman. Somehow she'd learnt the judge's daughter had run away and headed west. She'd learned the judge was desperate to get back his girl and that two men had died while trying to bring Lilly home. Broughton's pa had just been a pawn used by the devious Miss Clara. Rumble remembered her telling him, after he'd been put away, that he'd been a damn fool to allow himself to be framed for something he hadn't done, but even so she'd do her damnedest to get him out. She hadn't visited him again. He hadn't expected her to. Fact was he thought she'd forgotten him. He'd underestimated her. She'd used old man Broughton to put the idea into Thompson's head that Rumble was the man most likely to get the girl back.

Judge Thompson had swallowed the bait. He'd pulled strings to get Dennis Rumble out of the penitentiary. After speaking with the governess, Rumble was now aware that Thompson didn't give a damn about Lilly, but had a mighty compelling reason for wanting her brought home safe without anyone being any the wiser that she'd even gone missing.

'So you're following me West in search of a story,' he observed. 'You must be a damn fool, Miz Broughton.

We're heading into the badlands. There's a bunch of vicious owl hoots loose in this vicinity. They take delight in torture and murder.'

'Which you never did, Mr Rumble!' she snapped sarcastically.

'I never tortured anyone, Miz Broughton. I've taken no joy in killing. I've had to feed myself, clothe myself and put myself through school from an early age. When Ma died I was thrown out on the streets. I survived as best I could and did well for myself.' He fell silent. Miz Clara had told him he was an enterprising young varmint. But he guessed that even she, hardboiled as she was, had been shocked to find one so young so good at the job!

'You are damned, Dennis Rumble. You cannot justify what you did. You are destined for hell.' Harriett Broughton paused defiantly. 'And the only way you'll stop me getting my story is to kill me.'

He did not reply, preferring to ignore her foolish ramblings.

'And you might like to know that Captain Epson will be dealing with those murderous riff-raff. He is a man of decency, unlike yourself, Mr Rumble!'

'You're a fool, Miz Broughton. No decent man takes the heads of owl hoots he's killed and sets those heads upon posts to be photographed for good measure. And now I'd be obliged if you'd stop yapping.' He pulled his hat down over his eyes. Even Epson wouldn't dare set up a woman's head on a post, but he'd kill Miss Lilly if she'd ridden willingly, or even unwllingly, with the owl hoots. Epson was a fanatical law enforcer, to be brought in when others failed.

'You are a vile beast, Dennis Rumble.' She was

determined on the last word and so was he.

'Seems like I won't have to fight you off then, Miz Broughton,' he rejoined.

'How dare you. I am a respectable woman.'

He did not reply. Harriet Broughton could have the last word if only she would quit yapping. He had a hunch she was going to cause trouble but there was nothing he could do about her. Whatever she thought about him, he was not a crazed killer.

When Dennis Rumble left the stage at Poynton, Harriet Broughton likewise alighted. She held her valise in one hand. With the other she pressed a handkerchief against her nose. The place stank of horse dung.

Rumble, who was accustomed to the stink of fetid alleyways and the even worse stink that had permeated the penitentiary, strolled down the dusty main street in search of a hotel. He realized he looked out of place, for be was smartly dressed in Eastern garb: he also held a fancy gold-handled cane.

He sidestepped a pile of fresh horse-droppings. He turned his head when he heard a cry. Harriet Broughton had stepped in the mess.

'Now I know there is a God!' He didn't trouble to stifle a grin, knowing it would take her a while to figure out his meaning.

His gaze lingered on a group of youngsters down on their knees playing some sort of a game with a peg, each one taking a turn to move the peg with the end of his nose. As a youngster he realized he had never enjoyed such carefree games. Yep! He'd had other matters on his mind. He smiled grimly. Given the way the odds had been stacked against him he'd done darn well.

He'd heard that a certain Miz Clara had a problem with a certain well-connected man about town who'd threatened to shut her down. Rumble had marched up to her front door and offered her a deal. 'It will look like an accident,' he'd said. She hadn't been able to speak for laughing.

'Get out of my sight, you young varmint,' she'd yelled at last.

'I'll come back when I've done it. I'll want my money.' She'd stopped laughing then.

'You'll get yourself killed, boy,' she warned.

He had come back and she'd paid up, although she'd looked at him oddly.

'Any more jobs you want doing, Miz Clara, send them my way. I need the money!'

The jobs had snowballed. He only worked for women, reasoning that few of them could do the dirty work themselves. Miz Clara always acted as the go-between. Word got round. He always had an income. He'd always given his clients time to have a change of heart and sometimes they did. So far as he knew none of them had wanted him dead after the job had been done. He knew darn well Judge Thompson aimed to dispose of him once Miss Lilly was safely home.

The batwings of the saloon he had drawn level with burst open and a scrawny runt of an oldster ran out with surprising alacrity, almost crashing into him before the old man righted himself and had gone on, heading down Main Street as though the devil himself were on his tail.

Rumble stopped. And just as well, as he would have

been bowled over by the giant of a galoot who, whacking the batwings open with considerable force, emerged on to Main Street. Two things caught his eye, firstly the red-silk shirt that bulged over trousers secured by an elaborate silver buckle belt; secondly, the man's expression, which said he was enjoying himself.

'Damn potman,' the giant bellowed. His eyes beneath the thick eyebrows glared furiously around. They settled on the fancy-dressed stranger.

Rumble had a bad feeling about this. The man stank of liquor. He guessed that the stain on the red shirt was due to the old potman's clumsiness.

It was not Rumble's intention to become involved. He felt no desire to save the potman from the dangerous giant who had given pursuit. But, unfortunately, the fierce bloodshot eyes were staring in his direction! The potman was momentarily forgotten.

Rumble realized that it was his Eastern dress that had drawn attention his way. He realized he might be falsely giving the impression he was an easy target, an inoffensive Easterner who by now should be shaking in his boots.

'Trouble with you, Rumble,' a fellow inmate had told him, 'you don't look vicious. Them as don't know you take you for a weakling.'

'Just what the hell are you staring at, you damn peddler?' the man demanded aggressively.

Rumble knew he had not been staring. His eyes had purposely been fixed on a point beyond the speaker.

'Nothing at all, sir,' he replied mildly. He wasn't a proud man. He'd address all kinds of fools as 'sir' if it meant he could sidestep trouble. Violence, he had always believed, needed to serve a purpose. He didn't need to prove himself before the curious eyes of the spectators who'd stopped to see the show! Some looked gleeful; a few decent folk looked worried.

Harriet Broughton edged away. If Dennis Rumble were killed she could still write an article detailing the killing. 'He's the most dangerous and capable galoot you'll find to hire,' her pa had advised Judge Thompson. Rumble didn't look particularly dangerous, she thought dispassionately.

'Get off the street, ma'am, 'less you want to watch a man beat near to death,' a man hissed.

Harriet Broughton didn't move. 'I'm a reporter, sir,' she heard herself say.

'No you ain't!' Rumble corrected loudly.

'Come on now, Casper, let the man be. He means no harm.' The man who'd tried to get Harriet Broughton off Main Street spoke up.

'You get back behind your counter, storekeeper,' Casper snarled without glancing at the speaker.

Harriet Broughton pressed her handkerchief against her nose. Casper stank of liquor.

'Seems to me this quaking peddler is going to use Main Street as his toilet,' a bow-legged fellow yelled.

Rumble glanced at the speaker.

'How dare you, sir. There are ladies present,' Harriet Broughton cried loudly. There were murmurs of agreement from the other watching women.

The bow-legged galoot, Rumble noted, couldn't work out what he'd said to offend the womenfolk.

Rumble's tormentor spat. The gob of spit landed on Rumble's shoe. 'I can't abide a yellow-bellied coward,'

Casper bellowed. 'I can always smell them. And mister, you stink.' He paused. 'Now, I'm a reasonable man. I'm going to give you a chance to save your miserable hide. Get down on your hands and knees and crawl out of my sight.'

Rumble knew that the galoot aimed to plant more than a few kicks. He waited. He knew what was coming next.

'Guess I'm going to have to knock the stuffing out of you, peddler! You need to learn some manners.' The large fist clenched and a punch was swung.

Rumble had been waiting for this moment. His left fist came up out of his pocket as he sidestepped the blow, bringing his fist up to connect with Casper's chin. There was a sickening thud as blood and teeth spurted. But Rumble wasn't standing still. For good measure he planted his fist into the huge overhanging belly. The fight, if it could be called a fight, was over before it had started. His would-be tormentor fell to the ground, rolling in agony as he clutched his stomach.

'If anyone else wants a ruckus I am more than ready to oblige.'

'Hell, look what he's wearing on his knuckles. No wonder Casper's gone down without a fight!' someone bellowed.

'Mister, you've smashed Casper's goddamn jaw,' another observed in disbelief.

Rumble shrugged. He did not reply. He could have done far worse. Hell, he'd had more street fights than he could remember! And there'd been a few vicious fights in the penitentiary before inmates had learned to let him be. Spotting an approaching lawman, he wondered if there was going to be more trouble. With the lawman was the old potman.

'Get Casper over to the barber's,' the lawman ordered without preamble.

'I'll kill you mister. I'll kill you!' Casper gasped as he was helped away.

'Don't be a damn fool, Casper,' the sheriff warned. 'You cause any more trouble and I'll run you out of town myself. I've had a bellyful of you!'

'This stranger ain't fought fair,' the bow-legged little man who'd been eager to egg Casper on spoke up.

'No, he ain't. But he's avoided a stomping by Casper.' The lawman paused, 'And who might you be?' he demanded.

'The name's Yancey,' the man replied. Rumble sensed his reluctance.

'Well, Mr Yancey, get about your business. I peg you for a goddamn troublemaker.'

Yancey, lowering his head, walked away.

The lawman glared once more at Rumble. 'Stranger, don't stay around my town a mite longer than you have to. And you, saloonkeeper, I'm closing your establishment for today. You put up a closed notice. There ain't another drop of liquor to be sold until tomorrow. Liquor's behind Casper's viciousness!'

'You can't close the saloon.'

'Get the place emptied and closed up or I'll smash every goddamn bottle I can find. You folk clear the street. Get about your business. Don't make me throw any of you in jail. I'm the law in this town.' He eyed Rumble. 'I'm Sheriff John Sloan. I don't countenance trouble in my town. This time I'll concede it was forced upon you. And you are?'

'Dennis Rumble.'

'He's a felon,' a voice cried.

It was that goddamn woman Harriet Broughton. Fat face flushed with excitement, she approached the lawman.

'Are you two acquainted?' the sheriff asked curiously.

'Certainly not. I'm a respectable woman.'

'Well in that case, ma'am, I'd be obliged if you and the other respectable women would clear the street. When a fight looks apt to erupt the street is no place for a respectable woman, I'd say.'

'I'm a reporter.'

'Just clear the street, ma'am. There's a fine hotel at the end of Main Street.' He turned his attention to Rumble. 'Is what she says true?' he enquired with deceptive mildness.

'I've been pardoned, having been wrongly convicted of a killing that was not my doing,' Rumble replied easily. 'Check it out! I'm not heading out yet awhile.'

'If you ain't been pardoned we'll be having words. But right now I have more important matters to attend to.'

'Sheriff, you don't understand—' Harriet Broughto had decided it was her duty to warn the man he had a killer in town.

'Get off the street, ma'am, or I might think you ain't as respectable as you want me to believe.' Sheriff John Sloan had little time for women and their foolish chatter.

The vicious efficiency with which Rumble had dealt with Casper made it abundantly clear the man had done this kind of thing before. Sloan could only hope that the vicious varmint did not intend to stay in Poynton for any length of time!

But if it had not been Rumble, sooner or later Casper would have been bound to meet his match.

'You'll find out.' Harriet Broughton headed down Main Street in search of the hotel. The lawman, after giving Rumble a long cold stare, spun on his heels and strode away.

'Mr Rumble!' A voice stopped him in his tracks before he too could head for the hotel. It belonged to Higgins, a garrulous Irishman, a man from Rumble's past. He stifled a groan.

'It's good to see you, sir. Good to see you!' Higgins shook him vigorously by the hand. 'If there's anything I can do, anything at all? I'm your man! I was sorry to here about the bad luck which came your way.' When Rumble did not reply he continued, 'I never would have thought to see you in Poynton!' There was an expectant pause before Higgins concluded, 'Fact is, Mr Rumble, I am a man of property, for I own the Poynton livery barn.'

Rumble nodded. 'Just keep your mouth shut, Higgins, that's all I ask. I don't want folk knowing my business.' He hesitated for a moment. 'Upon reflection, I'd be obliged if you'd spruce yourself up and attend church service tomorrow.'

'Well, a man who runs a livery barn can't be expected to smell fresh,' Higgins rejoined, 'but I'll do it. I'll take a bath and dig out my funeral suit, the one I'm saving. Have you found religion, then, Mr Rumble?'

'No, you damn fool. I want you to point someone out for me.'

'And who might that be?'

'Just get yourself to church and keep your trap shut about what you know about me.'

'The only thing I know about you, Mr Rumble, is that you're a mighty fine gentleman. And like I said, I owe you plenty. But this town sure needs a man like you. That goddamn barber is nothing more than a butcher! He does his best but he ain't up to the task.'

'I ain't planning to stay around. I'm headed back East as soon as my business is concluded. Would you peg Sheriff John Sloan for an honest lawman? Do you think he'd throw in his lot with owl hoots?'

'Nope. But he ain't fool enough to go looking for the Coyotes. That's what the folk hereabouts call that murdering band holed up in hill country. Men fool enough to go after that bunch don't come back alive although some have come back in pieces.' Higgins stopped abruptly, his eyes narrowed thoughtfully before he bobbled away without saying another word.

Watching Higgins hobble away, Rumble knew that Higgins had worked out that a matter connected to the Coyotes had brought him West. But that knowledge at least Higgins would keep to himself. As for the rest, Rumble could not be sure. He checked into the hotel, then headed for the bathhouse, one place Harriet Broughton could not follow him. No respectable woman would set foot in the place.

Higgins kept an old table and a couple of chairs inside his livery barn. He'd caused a scandal when he'd bought the place because he'd employed a woman. Like Rumble he'd been raised the wrong side of the tracks and he'd survived because be knew people. He'd had a hunch that if he'd turned the widow away she was more than capable of setting about him with his own shovel. Unlike the women who'd hired Dennis Rumble, this one was more than capable of doing her own killing! Higgins had sensed her desperation and had known he was her last part of call.

She joined him at the table with a mug of hot coffee. Higgins sighed. She'd found his jug of liquor and thrown it out. He'd kept quiet, not wanting to rile her.

'Too bad about the sheriff's wife,' she declared, before adding, 'Looks like she's a gonner.'

'How so?' Higgins wasn't really interested. He listened with half an ear. 'I reckon Rumble could save her,' he muttered when a response was called for.

'But he's not here!' She hadn't troubled to see what the ruckus on Main Street was all about.

'But he is. He arrived today. Hell, I don't know what exactly has brought him West—'

'He's here – he can help.'

'He's here. But whatever his reasons for being in Poynton, helping folk ain't one of them. He won't want folk knowing his profession so don't go gabbing!'

But she wasn't listening. After snatching up a shotgun she dashed out of the livery barn. Higgins gaped after her.

'Say, mister, you're a mean-hearted varmint. You ain't the weakling I took you to be,' the bow-legged waddy was waiting outside the bathhouse. 'Why the hell didn't you kill him?'

Rumble eyed the man coldly. 'What I do is none of your

concern. Don't make it your concern.'

'No offence intended. Are you looking for work? My boss would hire a man like you, I am sure of it. I could put in a good word.'

'Hell, do I took as though I know the first thing about herding cows?'

'My boss can always use a good man,' the other persisted.

'I ain't interested. Make yourself scarce.'

Rumble spotted a large woman heading towards him. He also noted the shotgun. She did not look hostile but he had a hunch he would not like whatever she had to say.

'The sheriff's wife needs your help.' The woman blocked Rumble's path. She smelt of horses and he realized she was connected to Higgins. 'I know all about you. How you saved Higgins's leg when they were going to cut it off.'

'Now, ma'am, I really can't—'

She raised her shotgun. 'You can, Mr Rumble. You can.'

'Keep out of this, Yancey,' he advised. 'Or you'll be damn sorry,' he added warningly.

'You ain't wriggling out of doing your duty, Mr Rumble. I'm going to see you do right,' the woman declared.

'Ma'am, I ain't in Poynton because I want to do right.'

'Nevertheless you're gonna do right. Higgins has always spoken highly of you and that's good enough for me.'

'Sheriff John Sloan won't thank you for bringing me to his door, ma'am.'

Yancey trailed curiously behind the pair. He wasn't the only one to wander what the hell was going on. They were attracting a crowd. He knew damn well why Rumble hadn't jumped her. She was a respectable woman, after all. Out here men were obliged to treat respectable women with deference. Yancey smiled coldly. Unless they happened to run with the Coyotes!

CHAPTER 3

The sheriff, his Peacemaker drawn, emerged from his house. From inside there was a long-drawn-out scream. Blanching, Sloan kicked the door shut.

'What the bell is going on?' he roared gazing at the astonishing sight that confronted him. Miz Mattie evidently had brought Rumble here at the point of a shotgun.

'There's no need for profanity, Sheriff Sloan,' she snapped. 'You've been praying for help, haven't you? Well, here it is.' She jabbed Rumble in the back with the shotgun. 'This man,' her voice rose, 'this man is a doctor and a mighty fine one. This is the man who saved Higgins's leg! The Lord be praised, Sheriff, we can save your wife!'

'Have you gone mad!' the sheriff bellowed.

'No. It's true! Ask him '

'Are you a doctor? Can you save my wife?'

'I ain't interested in your wife,' Rumble prevaricated.

'Are you a doctor?' Sheriff John Sloan aimed his Peacemaker at Rumble's forehead.'

'I used to be.' Rumble paused. 'Before I was locked up

for murder. Now can I get about my business? This ain't my idea, as you can see. I was brought here under duress.'

'Higgins always said the doc who saved his leg was a miracle-worker,' Sheriff Sloan mused. 'But he never mentioned you by name.'

'And with good reason.' Harriet Broughton pushed her way through the crowd. 'This man is a monster! He financed his schooling by murder: from an early age Dennis Rumble supported himself by hiring out as an assassin. And he got away with it.'

'You know all about him!' Sheriff Sloan demanded. From inside his home came another scream.

'Indeed I do,' she replied self-importantly.

'What about his patients? What did they have to say about Doc Rumbler?'

'Ironically, he was highly regarded. They heaped praise upon his head. None of them knew they'd been in the hands of a fiend!'

'Hell! Doc Rumble always did his damnedest to save his patients. And those who couldn't pay well he treated plenty for free,' a voice yelled as Higgins shoved his way through the crowd. 'Why, there were plenty who wouldn't give a damn how he financed his tuition. Me for one! He saved my leg when the rest of the bunch wanted to saw it off!' He waved a bag. 'I've brought them. Old Doc Turpin's instruments.'

'Get inside, Rumble.' Sloan's voice was cold. There was a mad glint in the man's eye that Rumble did not care for. 'And you too, Miz Mattie.' The sheriff was a man at the end of his tether.

Inside, Sloan lowered his voice. 'My wife's going to die

unless she gets help. If you refuse to help I'll blast you.' He paused, 'If you help and she dies I'll blast you anyway. And I'll blast you too, Miz Mattie, for bringing this man to my door. That's how it's gonna be!' He waited expectantly, prepared for argument.

Rumble shrugged. Clearly Sloan was loco. 'I'll see what I can do. But I'm in charge. Cleanliness, Sheriff, that's what it's all about. Yep, there ain't nothing like carbolic and keeping folk who ain't never heard of carbolic away from the sick. We'll start by boiling the instruments. You see to it, Miz Mattie.' He eyed the sheriff. 'I hope you've got a strong stomach. You might need one!'

'This is a disgrace. Sheriff Sloan has lost his mind.' Harriet Broughton, left outside, shouted loudly. But she hesitated to bang on Sloan's door.

'Good thinking, ma'am,' the man Higgins advised. 'Right now Sheriff Sloan ain't in his right mind. He's been driven mad with worry. He might blast you for causing a disturbance and think about it afterwards.'

'So how many has the doc done for?' a waddy asked. 'Let me buy you a drink, little lady, and you can tell me all about it.'

Harriet Broughton struck him across the face. 'How dare you. I am a respectable woman.'

'You—'

'Back off.' Higgins had drawn a knife. 'Like this women said, she is a respectable woman even if she is a no-account gossip and a troublemaker. I ain't always been an ostler!' He paused. 'Me and Doc Rumble come from the same part of town. I hope you understand what I'm saying.'

'You crazy varmint.' The man backed away. 'I'll leave

you be because I don't care to have that crazy woman you employ on my tail. She's the one I'm scared of! Any man would be and that's a fact.'

Someone laughed and there were murmurs of agreement.

Higgins sheathed his blade. An ugly situation had been avoided. The quick-thinking varmint had backed down without losing face. 'Come along, ma'am. I'll escort you to the hotel,' he offered. 'Main Stteet ain't no place for a respectable woman like yourself right now.

'Very well,' she agreed. 'I've done my duty. The town now knows it is home to a monster.'

Higgins laughed, 'Old Doc Turpin was no monster but he was a drunken bum. We never found out who slit his throat but that would never happen to Doc Rumble. He ain't no bum and he ain't no drunk and he's a mighty fine sawbones. You won't find anyone to say different and that is a fact.'

Harriet Broughton sniffed. She ignored the man and did not even wish him good day once they reached the hotel.

Higgins, having got rid of the pesky woman, hurried back towards the sheriff's home. If Sheriff Sloan harmed a hair on Miz Mattie's head, Higgins had decided to slit the lawman open like a fish. That was, if Rumble didn't do it first. The lawman might believe he had the upper hand but Sloan did not know that Dennis Rumble, backed into a corner, was one mean varmint who wouldn't hesitate to cut the sheriff's throat before the lawman ever realized what Rumble intended.

Hell, why couldn't Miz Mattie have just kept her nose

out of a matter that did not concern her, the perplexed ostler asked himself? And for that matter, why had that damn troublemaker Harriett Broughton followed Doc Rumble West? He scratched his head. Why, there was even a female riding with the band of killers calling themselves the Coyotes. Idly he wondered whether Rumble's presence in Poynton had anything to do with the Coyotes. It was a long shot and did not seem likely because Rumble had only chosen to work for women, ones who'd wanted a husband or pa or brother removed. Yep, men could always resort to a compliant doctor and an asylum but the women? Well, their only resort had been Dennis Rumble, who'd obliged, it being understood the considerable fee only became payable once the job had been completed.

Rumble worked desperately to save Mrs Sloan. Twins were on the way if he were not mistaken. He felt oddly calm. Doctoring was what he did best. She was unconscious now. Yep, chloroform was mighty useful, Rumble reflected, reaching for his now scrupulously clean cutting tools. But the amount had to be judged with care, too much and they were done for, too little and they came round.

'Rumble. God help us,' Sheriff Sloan croaked.

'I know what I'm doing! And as for helping, that's your job, you and Miz Mattie,' Rumble advised as he raised a hand, the one which held the razor-sharp blade. Time stood still as Rumble worked on. Sloan felt as though he were going to pass out. There were just the three of them. Rumble had sent the townswoman who had been present packing.

'Here!' Rumble handed first one infant and then another to Miz Mattie. There was a moment's silence before the infants began to wail. For the first time Rumble smiled. 'Nearly done. It's early days but I reckon she'll be fine if my instructions are followed to the letter. Do you hear me, Sheriff Sloan? Cleanliness, that's what it's all about. I'll be in every day to check on Mrs Sloan. Now I'll just get stitching.'

'I owe you,' Sheriff Sloan croaked. 'And I don't mean money.'

'You don't owe me a damn thing.' Rumble didn't glance at the lawman.

'What that woman said—'

'I am a mighty fine sawbones, Sheriff Sloan. That's all you need to know. That and the fact I ain't a wanted man.'

Sloan sighed. He looked at his unconscious wife, whom this man had undoubtedly saved. 'I'm damned if I know what to think about you.'

Rumble smiled. 'Think the worst,' he advised. 'But it ain't my intention to stay in Poynton. You don't need to worry. I have a matter to look into and then I'll be on my way.'

'When we're satisfied Mrs Sloan is gonna be fine,' Sloan corrected grimly. 'Don't you try to leave town before then or I'll track you down.'

'I may need to take a ride directly after Sunday service. But I shall return to Poynton later in the day.'

Sloan nodded. He didn't enquire as to why Rumble might need to take a ride directly after Sunday service.

'What happened to your last doctor?'

'Someone slit his throat,' Sloan stated calmly. 'Doc

40

Turpin was a no-good drunken bum. I didn't waste time investigating.'

Rumble nodded.

'But if you don't come back after your Sunday ride sure as hell I'll track you down. I won't see it as a waste of time. Do we understand each other, Doc Rumble?'

Rumble nodded. 'I reckon we do. Now if you don't object I'll clean up and head for the hotel.'

There was a crowd of women still waiting outside the house. 'So how is Mrs Sloan?' one asked.

'She'll pull through. No visiting allowed until I give the word. Two fine boys if anyone is interested,' Rumble replied. His eyes narrowed. Yancey was still hanging around. 'Are you staying around town, Mr Yancey?' He sensed there was more to Yancey than met the eye.

'Nope. I'm a waddy, Mr Rumble. I've got chores to 'tend to.'

'From hereabouts?' Rumble essayed.

'Nope. My boss owns a spread just north of the town of Upstanding.' Yancey winked. 'Maybe we'll see you around. Are you sure you don't care to ride out with me? I don't reckon there is anyone hereabouts who could stop you!'

'Nope. Like you said, maybe I'll see you around.' Rumble moved away, aware that Yancey was watching him. Upstanding could wait. Tomorrow there was another matter he'd need to look into.

Whistling softly Rumble headed for church. He did not expect a warm welcome, but to his surprise half a dozen folk did greet him warmly.

Higgins, who was waiting outside, looked decidedly

uncomfortable in his suit.

'Point out the Mortimers when you see them,' Rumble advised softly. 'And be discreet.'

Higgins nodded. 'That's them! Do you see the big fellow with long grey hair? That's Mortimer! The woman with him is his wife. Now can I get back to my livery barn?'

'Where's the boy?'

'What boy is that, Mr Rumble? I ain't never seen Mortimer with any boy!'

Rumble eyed the couple. Nondescript was how he would describe them. They were farming folk dressed in their Sunday best. There was nothing interesting about the. Except there were two of them and there should have been three.

'Nope. We'll endure the service and then you can drive me out to their place. We'll follow them home!'

Cussing beneath his breath Higgins followed Rumble into church. He knew from the determined glint in Rumble's eye that he didn't have a say in the matter.

Sheriff Sloan, watching as Rumble and Higgins drove out of town, wondered what the hell was going on. So did Harriet Broughton. She knew that Rumble was a monster. Unfortunately, since he'd saved the sheriff's wife, folk in Poynton seemed kindly disposed towards him.

Higgins brought the buggy to a halt before the farmhouse. 'Is there going to be trouble, Mr Rumble?' he enquired mildly.

'If there is keep out of it. I'm only passing through this town. Seems to me you've taken root.'

Higgins shrugged. 'We've been spotted. They're

coming out and it seems to me Mortimer is prepared for trouble.'

'That's understandable,' Rumble agreed mildly. He saw the two still wore their churchgoing clothes. His gaze lingered for a moment on the shotgun Mortimer was carrying.

'What can I do for you gents?' the farmer asked without preamble.

'I want to see the boy you took in. The one the orphanage shipped out West about three years back,' Rumble stated bluntly watching carefully for Mortimer's reaction. He wasn't disappointed. Mortimer flinched.

'What's it to do with you, stranger?' Mortimer challenged.

'Let me see him. I want a word.'

Mortimer raised his shotgun. 'Get off my property. What the hell do you mean, coming here making demands, disturbing my day of rest!'

What happened next depended upon the kind of fighting man the farmer would turn out to be. There was an easy way to find out.

Rumble nodded. 'I've got the message. Easy with the shotgun. We're leaving.' He almost smiled at the man's very visible relief. 'Heh! Ain't that him at the window!'

As expected Mortimer, damn fool that he was, turned to look at the window and so did Mrs Mortimer.

The heavy wooden cudgel flew through the air and struck Mortimer with considerable force between his shoulder blades, causing the farmer to lurch forward, discharging his shotgun into the air as he fought to keep his balance.

Higgins was surprised the doc hadn't killed the man. He would only have needed to aim for the back of the man's head. And the doc's accuracy when throwing had always been good!

Rumble grabbed the shotgun and aimed it at the prone figure. 'Don't even twitch or I'll take off your head!' he yelled.

Mortimer continued to lie flat. He did not argue with the lunatic who had turned up at his door.

'Get his rifle,' Rumble ordered.

'Sure thing.' Higgins clambered down from the buggy.

'And keep your eye on Mrs Mortimer.' Rumble saw that the woman's face was contorted with rage. Unlike her husband she was not trembling in her boots. Perhaps because she thought, being a respectable female, that they would think twice before harming her, knowing the dire consequences they'd bring upon themselves.

'Get off our land, you no good varmints,' she yelled as she shook her fist. Spittle flew as she spoke. Of the two she was the one who posed the threat.

'You know why I'm here,' Rumble replied calmly. 'Whatever you're hiding ain't gonna remain hidden for much longer.'

'You varmint! We ain't hiding nothing. You've no business here, you meddlesome no-account!' Then, seemingly oblivious to the fact that Rumble was pointing a shotgun their way, she launched herself at her perceived tormentor.

He reacted instinctively. Reversing his grip on the shotgun he grasped the weapon by the barrel and struck out. The butt of the shotgun whacked hard against the side of Mrs Mortimer's face, hard enough to stop her in her tracks and send her howling to the floor.

'You fool woman! And you, Mortimer, get up. We haven't finished our conversation.'

Slowly the farmer got to his feet. He ignored his injured wife.

'Now, where's that boy? Spit it out while you've still got your to teeth,' Rumble encouraged.

'He's inside. We've got him locked in a cupboard,' Mortimer croaked. 'Just take him and get out of here. Leave us be. I never wanted him in the first place. It was all her idea. We'll get ourselves an orphan to help out with the work, she said!'

Mrs Mortimer groaned, tried to speak, then fell back on to the ground.

'Damn varmint. You've shattered the bone.' Mortimer cussed profusely, perhaps because his wife expected it of him. Or maybe he really cared about her.

Rumble spat. 'Get inside and find the boy,' he ordered Higgins. No matter how much he wanted to, he knew that it would be unwise to blast the two polecats. Any trouble he stirred up could impede his mission: the rescue of Miss Lillian Thompson, which of necessity must be accomplished before Captain Epson got his hands on her and hanged her!

Harriet Broughton watched curiously as the wagons trundled into town. As they were not attracting much attention she supposed they must be a common enough sight.

'They ain't nothing to worry about,' a female voice

observed. Harriet turned and stared at the creature who worked at the livery barn. 'Just workers for the mine,' the woman explained with a kindly smile.

'They are caged like lunatics,' Harriet observed.

'Just for their own good. It prevents any of them straying off,' Miz Mattie explained. 'They'll rest up here overnight and continue on tomorrow.' She paused. 'Say, do you know where Doc Rumble and Higgins might be headed?'

'Certainly not,' Harriet snapped.

'Thought you said you are a reporter.'

'I certainly am but that doesn't mean I'd converse with men such as Dennis Rumble.'

'I guess I'll find out. Our town needs a man like Doc Rumble. Too many folk have died on account of that useless varmint of a barber.' She paused. 'So have you come West to prove yourself, Miss Broughton?'

'I have come West to reveal the truth about Dennis Rumble. He's here for a reason. And as we both know, death follows in his wake.'

'No it don't. He saved the sheriff's wife. Higgins has always described him as a quiet, unassuming man except when he's riled. He's a mite unpredictable I'd say. And I guess he's a man who likes to keep out of trouble. I've heard tell he was none too keen to tangle with Casper but the confrontation was forced upon him.'

'He's a ruthless killer; more than that, he is a monster. But it seems folk in this town are prepared to set aside their principles in exchange for medical care!' Harriet Broughton sniffed. She watched as the men in charge of the caged wagons headed either into the saloon or the nearby eating-house.

'If it were up to the preacher he'd shut both saloon and restaurant on the sabbath but Sheriff John Sloan believes in live and let live.' Miz Mattie paused. 'Say, here they come no. Higgins and Doc Rumble. And they have a child with them.'

Higgins was relieved when Poynton came in sight. Rumble was seething with rage, and that both Mortimer and his wife lived said much for Rumble's self-control. It had been Higgins who had gone into the house and found the beaten and cowed child. It had been Higgins who had brought him out, wrapped him in a blanket and placed the boy in the buggy. Neither man had said much on the drive back to town.

'What the hell is this?' Sheriff John Sloan had clearly been watching out for Rumble's return.

'Hell, Sheriff, the Mortimers have been treating this youngster like a slave,' Higgins explained quickly. 'They ain't fit to have charge of him and have agreed that Miz Mattie is to have care of him for the time being.' He paused. 'I guess I'll be changing your duties, Miz Mattie. Doc Rumble here will employ you to take care of this young one till matters are settled.'

To his great surprise Miz Mattie, a curious expression on her face, merely nodded. Picking up the silent child she hurried away. 'You can count on me,' she called as she made herself scarce.

'Mortimer and his wife, they're alive and well,' Higgins volunteered before the sheriff could ask. 'Doc Rumble has not touched a hair on their heads.'

Sheriff John Sloan nodded. 'I am glad to hear that's so!' Rumble reminded him of a volcano set to explode. And right now Rumble was staring at the wagons on Main Street.

Without a word Rumble alighted from the buggy and headed towards the wagons. He had his principles, after all, the rules by which he lived, and he reckoned he was going to cause one hell of a ruckus as he gave Poynton the shake-up it needed.

He realized he did not give a damn.

CHAPTER 4

Yancey knew when to keep his mouth shut. Now was such a time.

'We've done well for ourselves boys,' the boss had said. And they'd all voiced their agreement 'We've had ourselves some fun and bagged ourselves a good deal of loot. But times are changing. There ain't a day goes by that civilization don't encroach a mite further. So, we're bowing out in style. Our last job is gonna make what we've taken seem like spare change. I've figured it all out. Now all you've got to do is trust me.'

As expected, all eyes had remained fixed on the man seated at the head of the table. They'd gathered together to share a pot of coffee, as was their custom, while the boss divulged what was in his mind.

'Bums!' he concluded much to the astonishment of them all, 'We need bums,' he reiterated. 'One for each of us. We need galoots without friend or kin. Galoots no one will miss; goddamn useless drunks who don't know one day from the next. Boys, you are headed out and each of you has gotta find one such bum, befriend him and bring him back here.' He paused. 'Steer clear of Poynton, do you hear me? We don't dirty on our own doorstep.'

'Sure thing, boss,' they chorused obediently, all except big Jimmy Mince who scratched the stubble that covered his chin.

'Hell!' he observed, 'It sounds as if you've gone loco, boss!' He guffawed, 'As crazy as a coot my old ma would have said.'

Yancey tensed immediately, aware that Jimmy Mince had crossed the thin line between familiarity and respect.

The boss didn't react immediately; eyes narrowing, he seemed to be considering big Jimmy's words. Then calmly, he picked up his mug of hot coffee and tossed the content into Mince's ugly face. With a howl big Jimmy sprang to his feet and, without thought of the consequences, acting solely from instinct, made the mistake of reaching for his Peacemaker.

The boss shot him mid-stomach. Mince, taking the chair with him, crashed to the floor, eyes glazing as unconsciousness overtook him. They all knew there was nothing they could do for the man and if he wasn't dead already he soon would be. No one moved except Yancey, who calmly continued to sip his coffee.

'I'd give my life for each and every one of you,' the boss told them, sounding as though he meant it. 'But I can't take disrespect from any of you. Disrespect leads to downfall! Jimmy Mince was a good man to ride with. We'll miss him but he overstepped the line.'

'Sure thing boss, sure thing.' No one disagreed.

'Of course, you men will share out big Jimmy's share of the loot.'

While the others grunted their assent Yancey poured another coffee. The boss's woman would have the job of cleaning up the blood now congealing around and under the late Jimmy Mince. And the bosss, Yancey was now sure, would have no hesitation in blasting the whole darn bunch of them without a qualm should the right time arrive. A cold shiver ran down Yancey's spine because Jimmy Mince had been right: the man seated at the head of the table was a loco son of a bitch. Maybe the boss was thinking that when the right time arrived he'd get rid of the whole damn bunch of them and keep the loot for himself. It was a chilling thought and worth chewing over, for Yancey's ambition was to die of natural causes.

'We'll see Jimmy off right,' the boss continued 'You men draw straws to see who'll dig his resting place. I'll read a few words from the good book to see him on his way.'

'He'll need more than a few words from the good book to help him where he's headed,' Fishwick, another of the crew, observed with a smirk.

The boss nodded. 'True, but, like I've told you, it's important to do things right and I reckon Jimmy Mince deserves a right send off. Does anyone think differently?'

No one did!

'Drink up and get digging,' the boss ordered. He paused before continuing, 'There are things afoot you men know nothing about. Leave the thinking and planning to me and I'll see you right!'

While the others murmured their agreement, Yancey kept his thoughts to himself. The boss was not the kind of *hombre* to see anyone right and that was a fact!

'So tell me about the new man in Poynton,' the boss ordered. 'I'm interested to hear about the new doc.'

Yancey shrugged. 'Word is he's a murderously inclined varmint, a galoot who has been murdering from an early age. It seems a certain Judge Thompson got him pardoned!'

'How do you know that?'

'There's a woman in town: a woman called Broughton. Seems her pa owns his own newspaper.'

'What's that got to do with her being in Poynton?'

'The damn fool woman claims she's a reporter.'

The boss snorted. 'Well, if she's right about Thompson being instrumental in getting the doc pardoned that can only mean he's been sent West to rescue Miss Lilly. That damn fool of a judge has already sent two no-accounts! Maybe he thinks third time lucky.' He smiled. 'The doc sounds an interesting galoot. I look forward to making his acquaintance.'

Yancey shrugged. 'He's a city man, boss, but he ain't a fool. Could be the varmint will be in no hurry to leave the safety of Poynton.'

'And maybe the doc will find Poynton ain't as safe as he might think it to be.' The boss smirked unpleasantly.

'What the hell is he up to now?' Sheriff John Sloan demanded impatiently. The doc, he saw, was seemingly engaged in conversation with the occupants of the cages.

'I'll give you a word of advice, Sheriff,' Higgins replied. 'Once the doc gets an idea into his head, once he's made his decision he cannot be dissuaded. He's a stubborn cuss who won't back down.'

'He's a monster, Sheriff, a monster!' Harriet Broughton shrilled. Both men ignored her.

'Furthermore,' Higgins continued, 'The doc don't much care for cages nor for them that keeps the keys to such cages. I'd say he's mighty put out seeing those cages on wheels standing bold as you please on Main Street as though they had every right to be there.'

'You seem to know a lot about him,' the sheriff essayed.

Higgins shrugged. 'The doc and me were never friends. But we grew up on the same streets. Our paths took different directions. Me, I'd leave those wagons be but that ain't the doc's way. He don't need or wants anyone to stand alongside him. He'll face this whole town if needs be!'

''So why are you telling me this?'

'I like you, Sheriff. You're a fair man for a lawman. Don't stand in his way!'

'None of us is safe while that monster is free.' Harriet Broughton did not trouble to lower her voice. 'Judge Thompson has a lot to answer for.'

Heading back towards the group on the sidewalk Rumble heard what she said. Harriet Broughton was a woman who could not keep her mouth shut. She'd tell anyone who would listen that it was Judge Thompson who'd got him pardoned. Whoever was running the Coyotes would hear the gossip soon enough. The man wouldn't need to be smart to figure out just why pardoned felon Dennis Rumble had headed West.

'So who is the boy?' Sheriff John Sloan asked when Rumble rejoined them. 'What are you doing with him?' He hoped to distract the loco doc.

Rumble ignored the lawman. 'Miss Broughton, have you been telling folk that Judge Thompson was instrumental in getting me pardoned?'

The startled expression on her face answered his question. 'Just get out of my sight, Miss Broughton, before I dump you in that horse trough yonder. Right now the sight of you riles me plenty.'

'Your threats don't scare me.'

'You're a damn nuisance. That's what you are, Miss Broughton! And if I hear another word from you I will dump you in that damn trough. Now keep out of the way. I reckon there's gonna be a ruckus.' He paused. 'Seems I'm the only one in this town to see what's wrong when it's before anyone's nose!'

'What nuckus?' the sheriff questioned. But he already knew the answer.

'I've given those unfortunate captives my word that they're gonna be set free.' Rumble paused. 'I reckon you'd best deputize me. What those galoots swilling rotgut whiskey inside the saloon are doing is against the law. Yep, you might be prepared to turn a blind eye but that ain't my way.'

'Why the hell should I deputize you?'

Rumble shrugged. 'There's always a slim chance that when confronted with a tin star the no-account varmints might see sense and back down, thus avoiding unnecessary violence. Take it from me those "prisoners" ain't headed for the Frobisher mine of their own free will.'

'How would you know?' Sloan demanded.

'I've asked them.' Rumble rattled off a sentence in a language the sheriff couldn't understand.

'Goddamnit, you're a doctor, not a lawman.'

'I'm a lot of things, Sheriff.'

'If you persist in this matter you'll bring grief on yourself and on this town. Frobisher won't let things be,' the sheriff warned.

Rumble shrugged.

'I've always kept trouble out of my town. You seem determined to bring it to my door.'

'You're deluding yourself. You ain't kept trouble out of your town. Trouble has stayed away of it's own accord. The Coyotes don't choose to raid in the vicinity of Poynton and no doubt Frobisher has instructed his men to be on their best behaviour whilst swilling beer and whiskey in Poynton. You've just been lucky so far.'

'If you walk into the saloon looking for trouble very likely you won't walk out again!'

Rumble ignored the remark. 'If you're running scared of Frobisher I can tell you right now that if that galoot comes looking for trouble I aim to take care of him.'

The sheriff's eyes were cold. 'I don't run scared.' He paused. 'I'll deputize you. You and me, well, we will see what we can do. Now raise your hand. We'll do this right. I'll swear you in. I'll let you play at being a lawman. Just for today!'

Rumble walked into the saloon. The place stank of cheap liquor and unwashed bodies mingling with the cloying perfume the saloon women liked to drench themselves with. He stood quietly and the piano player, catching his eye suddenly, ceased to pound the keys. Gradually the chatter ceased as folk began to realize trouble was brewing.

Frobisher's men had gathered together in a tightly knit group at the bar. Rumble knew their kind. He pegged them for well-trained dogs, extremely dangerous ones! Their raucous laughter was the last to die away. He didn't speak until he had their attention.

'You're gonna have to let those Chinese "slaves" you're toting to the Frobisher mine go. You're breaking the law. They ain't in those wagons of their own volition. So gentlemen, I'd be obliged if you'd pass over the keys.'

'You ain't no lawman.' It was the bartender who spoke up.

'I am. Sheriff John Sloan has sworn me in.'

'What's your handle, you no-account piece of garbage?' the leader of Frobisher's men snarled.

'I'm Dennis Rumble. And you are?'

'I'm Joe Morgan. And the sight of you makes me want to vomit. I can't abide meddlesome do-goods.'

Dennis Rumble smiled. 'That's the first time anyone has ever called me a do-good.' He paused. 'Go right ahead and spew up but hand over the keys first.'

'The hell I will. You jumped-up tin star.' Joe Morgan withdrew a ring of keys from his pocket and dangled them from the fingers of his right hand.

'Just do as the deputy says and hand over the keys!' Sheriff John Sloan barked the order. 'And tell Frobisher to steer clear of Poynton. The deputy is right. You've been breaking the law. I don't want to see any more of the slave wagons in my town!'

'Well, it's easy to see who is running this show and sure as hell it ain't you, Sheriff John Sloan,' Morgan said with a sneer.

The lawman ignored the insult.

'The town ain't with you on this matter, Sheriff.' This time it was the storekeeper who'd decided to speak up. 'Hell, what's gotten into you, Doc Rumble? This ain't your concern.'

'He's a doc!' Morgan stared in disbelief. Then he grinned. 'Well, in that case I won't stomp the stuffing out of him. Hell, Sheriff! I know your heart ain't in this. I'll take the wagons and head out to Frobisher's mine. And we'll make sure to steer clear of Poynton on future runs.'

'That sounds fair enough.' An elderly man spoke up. Others murmured their agreement.

Joe Morgan grinned. 'Too bad, doc! You've been outvoted. Folk in this town know better than to bring down grief upon themselves: Norman Frobisher ain't a forgiving man.' His grin broadened. 'And I'd suggest, Doc, that if the sight of those wagons offends your sensibility you don't look. Keep your nose out of what's not your concern.' A gob of chewing baccy that Morgan had been enjoying landed on the toe of Rumble's boot. Someone laughed.

Watching Rumble the lawman realized that the man didn't give a damn about the baccy or being seen as an object of derision. But he also realized that it was indeed true that once the doc had made up his mind to see something through he would not back down. Nevertheless Sloan was caught off guard when Rumble took action.

The doc didn't speak but reacted without warning. He'd walked into the saloon carrying his fancy cane and now he used it. And from the quickness of the movement Sloan realized that the man had done this before. The long concealed blade was withdrawn from its casing. Rumble's arm moved. The blade swished down and Joe Morgan uttered a scream of pain. He kept right on screaming as something fell to the floor. But by then Rumble had stepped forward and the tip of his sword had come to rest on the mid-belly of one of Morgan's pards.

'Anyone twitch and I'll run him through,' the doc yelled.

'Hell!' The lawman raised his shotgun and covered the group. 'Back off, Rumble, I've got them covered'

The doc stepped back and retrieved the keys.

'The town ain't with you on this, Doc Rumble,' the storekeeper babbled.

'Lord save me from fools!' Rumble exclaimed. 'Do I look as if I give a damn what this no-account town thinks. Best run these no-goods out of town, Sheriff. If they get in my way I'll kill them.'

Writhing on the floor Morgan let rip with a string of profanities as the bartender, keeping a careful eye on the loco doc, came out from behind the bar with towels to wrap the bleeding remains of the man's fingers.

'Get moving, gents. It's time you left town.' Keeping them covered the lawman shepherded the bunch towards the batwings.

Following the lawman, Rumble spotted the three men who had emerged from the eating-house.

'Rein them in, Morgan,' he ordered. 'A bloodbath on Main Street won't trouble me none,' he encouraged.

But it was the sheriff, not Morgan, who yelled out the warning not to haul iron. After a moment's hesitation they complied.

'Now Frobisher has done wrong,' the lawman advised them. 'He's broken the law and I guess he's doing so out at the mine. But I don't plan to come calling. If he's a wise man he'll leave things be and keep away from Poynton. The workers he's lost here today can easily be replaced.'

'That damn do-good will pay,' a man replied as he helped a moaning Joe Morgan on to a now empty wagon. 'And at the best you're gonna find yourself out of a job, you gutless—'

He got no further as the butt of the sheriff's shotgun connected with the side of his head. 'You damn fool,' the lawman cussed. 'I've saved your hides. Our loco doc is more than capable of killing the whole bunch of you. That's the kind of man he is. He's in the same category as Norman Frobisher except I guess he sees things a mite differently. But he is just as lethal. Now I want the whole bunch of you varmints out of my town!'

As soon as they were gone he would take back the tin star. If Dennis Rumble was crazy enough to pay Frobisher's mine a visit be could do so without a star to back him up. Sloan had always been aware that the place ran more or less on slave labour. But nobody in Poynton had given a damn as the mine had brought money into town.

'Dump your weapons before you ride out!' the lawman ordered. 'I ain't fool enough to take a chance on any of you taking a few pot shots as you are leaving.' The lawman sensed that the crew were still undecided. 'You men are loyal to Frobisher. I know that. I respect you for it. But those wagons ain't worth dying for. Now dump the weaponry and ride on out. I'll see it is returned at a later date.'

To his relief Frobisher's men, grumbling and cussing, complied.

'What the doc has done will cost this town.' The storekeeper had joined the lawman, 'The town council ain't going to be pleased with this.'

The lawman sighed. 'This town has been shaken up for sure. Maybe we needed an outsider to make us see wrongdoing can't be ignored on account of profit. Now get about your business.'

'And your business is that mine, Sheriff,' Rumble advised when the two were alone. 'The time has gone when you can ignore just how Frobisher has made his profit. If you don't get round to the place then I must.'

'Frobisher is a hard man,' the lawman observed. 'And he's vicious. He does not like to be crossed. You won't have heard the last of this, Rumble. He'll bide his time and when an opportunity to get even presents itself he'll take it.'

Rumble shrugged.

'You didn't come West to lock horns with Norman Frobisher, now did you?' The lawman was now clearly fishing.

Again Rumble shrugged.

'You've been lucky so far, I reckon,' Sloan continued. 'But one of these days your luck will run out.'

CHAPTER 5

At first sight Norman Frobisher, a tall thin man with sandy hair and spectacles perched on the end of a long thin nose, seemed more suited to teaching school than owning and running a highly profitable mining operation.

'You've let me down, Joe,' Frobisher informed an ill-at-ease Joe Morgan.

'I've told you, boss, the doc's loco.' Joe Morgan winced. 'My hand is hurting like hell!'

Frobisher poured another generous helping of whiskey. 'Drink up,' he encouraged. 'It'll ease the pain.'

'Sure thing boss.' Morgan downed the fine imported whiskey. 'I'll be as good as new if I can just rest up some,' he whined, taking hope from the fact that the boss seemed to have taken the bad news better than he had expected.

'You've let me down, Joe, and that's a fact,' Frobisher stated with enforced calmness. Right now he wanted to hammer Joe Morgan's stupid face until it was unrecognizable. But he could not be seen to be losing control. However, he knew just how to hammer Joe, theoretically speaking. 'And the fact is, with a maimed gun hand you can't pull your weight around here. Hell, Joe! The fingers on your right hand ain't much more than stumps.'

Realization dawned. 'You ain't firing me, are you, Mr Frobisher? I've served you well all these years—'

'With one month's salary in lieu of notice. Brown and Johnson will escort you off my property.'

'But—'

'I've no choice Joe. Our workers have to believe we're invincible. That's what keeps them toeing the line. Now the sight of an overseer with his fingers part-sliced off, that's liable to make them start thinking and that can only be bad. I'm sorry, Joe, but you've got to go.'

There was a knock at the door. At Frobisher's command the two men just mentioned entered. Removing their hats in Frobisher's presence they waited for orders.

Frobisher stood up. The talking was over. There was nothing more to be said. 'Collect your money and get the hell off my property!' He shook his head. 'Like I've told you. You've disappointed me. You're not the man I thought you to be.'

Joe Morgan swallowed but kept silent. He knew what Frobisher riled was capable of. Maybe that was why the notorious Coyotes had left the mine alone. And if they had more sense than to stir up Norman Frobisher then so did he. He nodded.

Frobisher turned away. He waited until the door had closed behind the three men before picking up the empty whiskey bottle. Deliberately he smashed it with great force against the table, sending shards of glass flying in every direction.

He wanted to round up his crew and descend upon Poynton. He wanted to drag the doc, the man named Rumble, out of the two-bit town. And then he wanted to inflict whatever atrocities he could think of on the man who'd crossed him. He'd been humiliated. No one humiliated Norman Frobisher with impunity.

He began to breath slowly, knowing that control was everything. He could not be ruled by impulse. He could not openly challenge the rule of law in Poynton, because if word got out, as it would, he'd be ruined. He would no longer be regarded as a respectable businessman who could be trusted with funding. He'd be seen as a crazed renegade, no better than the scum known hereabouts as the Coyotes. The respectability that he'd worked so hard to achieve would be in jeopardy. So for now he must bide his time. He could be patient when he had to be. Dennis Rumble would pay for meddling, and as for Sheriff John Sloan, that galoot wasn't worth a spit. But for now he wasn't bothered with Sloan.

Opening his door he yelled for the old crone who cleaned up to sweep up the glass and put the sweepings on the table. There they would stay until he could force them down Rumble's throat.

'Hell, Joe! What a pickle! This Doc Rumble must be one crazy galoot,' Brown commiserated with Morgan.

'You'll land on your feet, Joe,' Johnson likewise encouraged. 'Say, I know a galoot down in border country who owes me a favour. You tell him Johnny Johnson sent you and you'll have a job.' He proceeded to rattle off directions.

'Much obliged. I'll look him up '

'I guess we've gone far enough. Good luck, Joe.' Brown reined in his horse. 'Be seeing you Joe. Best of luck, pard.'

'Sure thing, boys. See you around.' Joe Morgan rode on. He did not look back.

Brown watched through narrowed eyes. Then, drawing his rifle he sighted the weapon upon its target. He knew Joe Morgan, damn fool that he was, would not look back. The slug hit Morgan mid-back, breaking the spine. Morgan fell from the saddle as his terrified horse took off.

'Damnation!' Johnny Johnson cussed. 'Now you and me have got to retrieve that horse.' Joe Morgan's boots were still caught by the stirrups and Morgan's head was being smashed to pulp by the bolting horse. 'Hell, Brown, why did you have to backshoot him whilst he was in the saddle? Why not just make him dismount like I wanted?'

Frobisher had told them to help themselves to whatever money might be in Joe's pockets.

'Like I told you, we've worked with the galoot. This way he wouldn't have known what was coming his way. Just because we do Frobisher's dirty work don't mean we're lacking in decency.' He warmed to his theme. 'There's killing and killing, Johnny. Don't you forget that Joe was one of us! His luck just ran out, that's all.'

'Damn fool! He ought never have come back whining how this loco doc got the drop on him.' Johnson shrugged. 'Let's get on with it then.' He dug in his spurs and set off in pursuit of the runaway horse. 'Hell,' he grumbled, 'there's no telling where this ruckus with the loco doc is liable to lead.'

Brown spat out a plug of chewing tobacco. 'It'll only

end one way. That meddlesome varmint will regret the day he crossed Boss Frobisher. He'll be begging for a gun to be put to his head by the time Boss has finished with him.'

Richard Kent, boss of the Lazy R ranch, lit a cigar. He smiled indulgently at the woman seated at the far side of the comfortably furnished room.

'Seems that loser your pa dispatched west to "rescue" you ain't in a particular hurry to fulfil his commission.' He drew on the cigar. 'Tell me, Lilly, why the hell is your pa so damn anxious to get you back?'

Lillian Thompson poured herself a glass of whiskey. She held his gaze for a moment. 'Like yourself, Richard, my pa is a vengeful man. I crossed him by running off. My pa doesn't like to be crossed.'

Richard Kent smiled unpleasantly. 'For now you can keep your secrets, my dear. Maybe this third loser will know. Maybe he'll spill the beans before I send him to meet his Maker bawling and begging for mercy. You can have a ringside seat. What do you say?'

Lillian downed her drink. 'You ain't thinking straight!'

'How so?' he enquired with deceptive mildness.

'The man's a doctor. You must curb your impatience to settle this matter. We may need him after all. Yancey spoke highly of him.'

Richard Kent nodded. 'It's hard to figure out what the crazy varmint is liable to do next.'

He had sent his man Fishwick to Poynton with instructions to keep out of trouble and watch the doc until there was anything to report. Fishwick had returned sooner than had been expected with details of the ruckus with Norman Frobisher's men. Kent knew that by crossing Frobisher the doc had made a deadly enemy. Fishwick had also reported that the doc had removed a youngster from the care of sodbusters named Mortimer before returning to the subject of the doc and Norman Frobisher.

'Word is,' Fishwick had reported, 'folk in Poynton seem to think the doc is loco enough to head out to Frobisher's mine and have it out with Boss Frobisher. Of course there ain't none of them crazy enough to ride with him, especially not Sheriff John Sloan.'

'Clearly he doesn't know where the Coyotes are based,' Lilly had later observed. 'And he'll know that word of my pa being instrumental in his release will have spread, meaning the Coyotes will be watching out for him. But that don't mean he's afraid. It means Doc Rumble has decided to play a waiting game. Meanwhile he's making a show of filling Doc Turpin's shoes.' She downed another whiskey, knowing that she was still alive because life had taught her to play the chameleon. Obliged to watch Richard Kent's savageness she'd urged him on to greater wickedness where another woman would have screamed and sobbed. He'd been impressed so he'd kept her around. Staying alive was what it was all about and she didn't care what she had to do to save herself.

'I'm damned if I know what's going on in that head of yours,' Richard Kent complimented. She'd just shrugged when he'd speculated where the Mortimers fitted into the picture. Now he smiled, a real goddamn smile of pleasure. 'Hell, it's all coming together better than I could have foreseen. The devil can take Doc Rumble but not before he's served his purpose.' Abruptly his mood changed; he picked up the empty whiskey bottle and hurled it at the wall. 'Goddamnit, how long does it take to round up a few bums?'

'Not just any bums,' Lillian soothed. 'We need particular kinds of bums. And the more addled with liquor they are the easier it will be to control them. We don't want any mistakes, not now, not ever.'

'Hell, anyone would think you've taken over the running of the outfit.' He grinned unpleasantly. 'Don't fool yourself. Without my protection those men would be on you like a pack of mad dogs.' When she did not rise to the bait he continued, 'And speaking of mad dogs, that brings me back to Rumble. He's a goddamn fool. We know that, or he would not have come West. And now he's riled Frobisher. That's good. We can use it to our advantage. Lilly, there ain't no help for it but I must forgo the pleasure of dispatching Rumble myself. Frobisher can have that pleasure, courtesy of the Coyotes.'

'Just what have you got in mind?' Lillian Thompson cooed, knowing her survival depended on playing up to Kent. Indeed, she was inclined to think that Dennis Rumble would go the way of his predecessors. She had watched as they had been killed. It had not been pleasant but she had discovered she had the stomach for such matters.

Dennis Rumble honed his blade. Sooner or later Casper was sure to make a move. He wished it could be sooner rather than later but the code by which he lived prevented him from goading Casper into confrontation. Casper's own free will would prompt the man into making that fatal error of judgement in thinking himself capable of dispatching Dennis Rumble.

For now the man was contenting himself by directing a malevolent eye in Rumble's direction whenever their paths crossed out there on Main Street. Yep, Casper reminded him of a mangy cur hanging around a haunch of meat, desperately wanting a bit but to fearful to dash in and take a chunk. But sooner or later Casper, metaphorically speaking, would make that fateful dash. And when he did he would leave this world in not maybe the best way to make an exit.

Higgins entered the surgery, hat held uncomfortably between his dirt-begrimed hands.

'Spit it out. What have you done,' Rumble demanded without preamble, aware that Higgins was not one to pay a social call.

'Well, I reckon you'd best hear it from me,' Higgins muttered. 'Not that you're likely to go loco. That ain't your way, I recollect.'

'Which makes me think you think I will go loco.' Rumble eyed the ostler and realization dawned. 'Hell, it ain't you is it, Higgins? It's Miz Mattie! What's she done now? Hell, it ain't nothing to do with the boy, is it?' He hadn't given the rescued youngster much thought. He'd assumed the widow was taking good care of the boy.

'Hell no. Miz Mattie dotes on that boy.' Higgins fidgeted. 'Fact is she's gone and taken in Miz Harriet Broughton. Seems old man Broughton has cut off her funding and instructed the sheriff to put her on a stage East. The hotel threw her out, she won't take a stage East and so Miz Mattie took her in. Seems she thinks Miz

Broughton will be useful to have around.' He waited expectantly but to his surprise Rumble did not evince rage.

'Why would Miz Mattie think Broughton would be useful to have around?' Rumble queried.

'What are you gonna do?' Higgins asked.

'Nothing. Sooner or later Harriet Broughton will head back to her pa.'

'I don't reckon Miz Mattie aims to let you take that boy back,' Higgins volunteered unhappily. 'So I'm telling you now, Doc Rumble, that if it comes to it I feel obliged to side with Miz Mattie. We've reached an impasse, Doc Rumble.'

'Don't think I won't dispatch anyone who crosses me, even you, Higgins.' Rumble sighed. 'But right now I can't rightly predict how the cards are gonna fall, so I suggest you get back to shovelling muck out of your livery barn.'

Higgins carefully backed out, trying to hide his relief. Rumble resumed his methodical honing of his blade. He knew damn well that Harriet Broughton would be rooting around for whatever information she could put into her fool story; not that her pa, old man Broughton, would be fool enough to print anything Harriet came up with. With that in mind an apparent problem was not a problem at all. And, like he'd told Higgins, he could not say how the cards would fall. For now he was obliged to play a waiting game.

He found himself wishing those goddamn Coyotes would make a move. There'd be a certain satisfaction in dealing with that murderously inclined bunch of deviants.

*

If she had had anywhere to go apart from back to her pa, Harriet Broughton would have walked out of the hovel inhabited by Miz Mattie.

'It don't matter how smart you are, Miz Broughton, your pa ain't never going to hand over control of his paper to you.'

Harriet ignored the woman.

'You got any kin?' Miz Mattis demanded.

'A cousin, I believe.'

'You believe? Either you know or you don't know.'

'Yes. I have a male cousin.'

'There you are. Your pa will never trust you with the paper if there's a male relative around. What you need is a husband, Miz Broughton. You'll find life easier. Me, I aim to marry Higgins but he does not know it yet.'

'I beg your pardon?'

'He can provide for me and the boy. He ain't so bad!' She hesitated. 'There's one hell of storm brewing. Men are gonna die before this is over. I sure hope Higgins don't get caught up in matters that are not his concern.'

'What matters?'

'Whatever matters that have brought Doc Rumble to Poynton. Whatever matters he chooses to make his concern.'

'Is that why you won't sleep at night, Miz Mattie?' Harriett asked carefully.

'Vigilance,' Miz Mattie replied, 'is called for.'

Miz Mattie, Harriet noticed, was staring at the axe kept very near to their front door. There was an odd expression on her face.

And then Miz Mattie laughed. 'No need to be afraid,

Miz Broughton, it ain't you that needs chopping. I'll see to the kindling then show you how to make up a fire. I know you want to earn your keep. And quit trying to dig up dirt on Rumble. He ain't as bad you think. He's saved the boy. I never knew those damn Mortimers had taken in an orphan and those who did forget the fact.' She gave a sniff. 'No matter what Rumble says I aim to keep the boy and raise him as my own.'

At last the waiting was over and Richard Kent could start wheels turning. He'd received the missive for which he'd been waiting. And Miss Lilly had come up with a few excellent ideas that he would never have thought of himself. She'd told him she knew just how to deal with mad dogs.

He offered Yancey a cigar. 'You tell the men I much appreciate their good work.'

Coyotes and dogs were not dissimilar, Lilly had jested.

'Sure thing, boss.' Yancey felt the boss was enjoying a private joke. 'I'll smoke this later.' He did not presume to sit and smoke in the boss's presence. He was mindful of how overfamiliarity had done for Jimmy Mince, a man who despite his outspokenness, had always been loyal.

'So how are the bums faring,' Kent enquired casually. 'Any of them got round to kicking up a stink?'

Yancey permitted himself a smile. 'As to that, boss, the varmints sure as hell stink. Just being anywhere near them makes me want to vomit, but as for kicking up a stink, why, those witless fools think they are in heaven, all the booze they can get down and the promise of obliging women.'

'Good. Now I've a special kind of job for you, Yancey, an

important one, so don't let me down. I'm counting on you.'

Yancey listened without comment. He did not care for what he was hearing but ever mindful of what had befallen Jimmy Mince he kept his trap shut.

'Sure thing boss,' he agreed readily when his boss had finished speaking.

To his mind what the boss required did not make any kind of sense. The doc was best left be. Rumble could be one hell of a problem. As for the woman, well, she was just a female after all, and females froze like rabbits ready for the slaughter, as he and the Coyotes well knew. The only exception they had ever encountered had been Miss Lilly, and it had been this uniqueness that had kept her alive. The boss had been taken with her right from the first.

Kent watched as Yancey swaggered out. He liked Yancey. Not that this was worth a damn. Like the rest of the bunch, Yancey was expendable. He smiled; pretty soon he'd be living like a king of the world.

Casper skulked in an alleyway. It stank of rotting garbage. The big man ignored the stink; the only garbage he was interested in right now answered to the name of Rumble. For the past few days he had not touched a drop of liquor. He knew that he needed a clear head and a steady hand for Rumble to be given his just deserts.

The town slept now. Sheriff John Sloan had made his last round, the last few customers had staggered from the saloon. The livery barn doors were barred. Casper clenched his huge fists and tried to dredge up stomach for what must be done. Rumble had bested and belittled him before the eyes of the town. Casper had heard folk snigger behind his back. Above all he wanted to show them what happened to those that crossed him and yet still he hesitated: the voice of reason which would not be stilled warned him that Doc Rumble was pure poison and best left alone.

Stiffening his shoulders, he took that first step towards his target and then froze as the night air carried the barely audible sound of riders heading into town. That they were riding in at this late hour signified that the varmints were up to no good.

He could just about make out the shapes of four riders. As they headed down Main Street he realized the hoofs of their horses had been wrapped in cloth to deaden sound. They stopped beneath a freshly painted shingle that simply read 'Doc Rumble'. That these men intended to snatch Doc was glaringly obvious.

Casper retreated cautiously backwards, settling himself down behind a pile of stinking pillage. If his presence were discovered they'd kill him. From somewhere outside of town a coyote howled which made Casper wonder whether these men were in some way connected to the murderous bunch calling themselves the Coyotes. He kind of hoped they were because men caught and killed by the Coyotes did not die easy. If Doc Rumble were to suffer a painful and protracted death that suited Casper just fine.

'Me and Nash will deal with the boy. You two see to the doc,' Yancey ordered.

'Nope,' Fishwick replied mildly. 'Me and Clemence ain't going after that loco doctor. We'll see to the boy. You and Nash can deal with the doc.'

'Now, listen, you no account bum,' Yancey hissed, 'I'm the one giving the orders.'

'Not right now you ain't! I aim to die with my boots off!' Fishwick stood his ground knowing Yancey would not risk a ruckus here and now. 'The boss ain't exactly said which two of us are to get the boy and which two are to grab the doc! I ain't budging on this and that's a fact!'

'Go get the boy.' Yancey had no choice but to capitulate. He could not risk a ruckus. Speed was damned important. 'It seems to me that all you two bums are good for dealing with is an old woman.'

'She's still mighty strong,' Nash volunteered. 'Hell, you ought to see her shovelling out the livery barn.'

'Then these two no-account bums best keep their wits about them,' Yancey jibed.

'The boss said she ain't worth a spit,' Fishwick rejoined. 'If she so much as croaks I'll wring her scrawny neck.'

His companion Clemence chuckled softly as the two riders veered east, keen to get on with the job before Yancey changed his mind.

'Damn varmints,' Yancey muttered. 'I know for a fact the boss would prefer she ain't harmed. Harming a respectable female tends to rile folk' He smiled. 'Naturally, the other kind don't count.'

Nash shrugged. 'So much the better. If they harm the old biddy they'll stir up a hornet's nest. The boss will be riled plenty. Maybe they'll go the way of Jimmy Mince.'

Yancey spat 'That's too much to hope,' he rejoined sourly.

Fishwick and Clemence stopped before the dark shape

of the house. 'Remember,' Fishwick hissed, 'If there's a ruckus over at Doc's place we fork it out damn quick. To hell with the boy, I say.'

'You sound as if you're expecting trouble?' Clemence essayed.

'Maybe. But if anyone gets dispatched tonight it ain't gonna be us.'

CHAPTER 6

Loud snoring broke the silence. Miz Mattie sighed. Harriet Broughton, whom she had taken in to help out during the day, snored like a hog. But leastways, having Harriet around gave Mattie a chance to snooze during the day.

She had a gut feeling that the boy was part of the jigsaw. He was involved in whatever had brought Rumble West. However, now that the youngster was safe and being well cared for, Doc Rumble appeared to have lost interest. But maybe there were others interested in the child. And if they sought to remove him from her care, well, she was more than ready to deal with them. She knew what needed to be done and, more important, knew that she was capable of doing it.

While Harriet Broughton continued to snore Mattie sat in the darkness, comfortable in her old sagging chair, freshly sharpened axe within easy reach. These were dangerous, lawless times. And the frontier was not a place for weaklings.

When she heard the window creak slightly and felt the flesh night air she wasn't surprised. She'd been expecting something, if not this break-in then something else. Her hand closed over the axe handle. It was cool to the touch and the feel of the wood against her palm she found comforting.

Whoever the fool was, who was breaking into her place, he cleanly didn't know her very well. Women were expected to freeze with fear when confronted with adversity but she had never done what had been expected. Very likely whoever was breaking in would be prepared to kill the two women should they get in the way.

Fortunately Harriet snored on. By the time she woke it would all be over, Mattie thought as she prepared for what had to be done to save the three of them.

'Hell!' Clemence observed in a loud whisper, 'I ain't had a woman in a long time. Even old Mattie would feel good in the dark. What do you say?'

'I say put the idea out of your head. We do exactly what the boss ordered. We're to leave the old biddy be unless she causes a ruckus and that ain't likely. My fist will see to that.'

'Hell, the boss—'

'Quit arguing, Clemence! We'll do this right, like we've been ordered.' There was a soft grunt as Clemence's pard, whoever he was, came through the window. 'You pass that goddam chloroform, then get your butt in here.'

A snore broke the silence. 'Damn it, old Mattie snores like a hog!' Fishwick hissed as he too entered Mattie's house. As his eyes adjusted to the gloom he paid no attention to the high-backed chair facing away from the window, a shape in the gloom. 'You grab the boy while I deal with the old woman,' he ordered.

Her hand tightened on the axe handle. She was furious

now, hearing herself dismissed with insult. She waited until they had passed her chair before she came silently to her feet. She'd always been a strong woman. She'd used her strength when she worked shovelling out at Higgins's livery. The axe was damn heavy but it didn't give her any trouble as she raised it and brought it down with ferocious fury.

Clemence, sensing a presence in the darkness, began to turn as the axe thudded into his skull, splitting his face almost into two halves.

Fishwick dropped the chloroform-soaked rag and reached for his Peacemaker. The axe took his hand off at the wrist before he could fire even one shot. He screamed, a long-drawn-out howl of agony as blood spurted.

He was dying from the lost blood, was about to lose consciousness, but Mattie in a fury continued to lash out, her axe thudding into the man again and again.

In the bedroom Harriet Broughton sat up. 'Murder!' she screamed.

Miz Mattie dropped the blood-soaked axe and lit a lamp. 'You stay put, Miss Broughton,' she yelled. 'This is no sight for a gentlewoman.'

Across Main Street Yancey heard the piercing scream. He'd been steeling himself to enter Rumble's surgery. When it had come down to it he'd unexpectedly balked at carrying out the task of snatching Doc Rumble. The man was a prolific killer, after all, if Harriet Broughton were to be believed. Nor was Rumble a fool, as his boss seemed to think.

'Mount up, Nash, we're forking it our.' Yancey's gut

feeling told him to get the hell out of town this very instant.

Nash didn't need urging. He swung into the saddle almost as quickly as Yancey. Digging in their spurs the two men forked it out of Poynton as lights began to appear at darkened windows.

Watching from the mouth of the alleyway, Casper spewed out a string of profanities. Once again the Devil had taken care of his own. Rumble had escaped whatever was due to come his way.

'Hell!' a voice bellowed. 'It's Miz Mattie! She's gone mad.'

Inside the surgery Rumble heard voices yelling about Miz Mattie having gone crazy. He'd been expecting Casper this night but it had been the Coyotes who'd made their move. And they'd gone after the boy! He'd been a fool. But thank the Lord for Mattie.

He'd recognized the muffled voice from beyond his window. He'd known Yancey and another was out there. He'd known they were coming for him. Indeed he'd been debating whether to keep Yancey alive. There'd be plenty of interesting information that Yancey would have divulged with a little persuasion, but the choice had been taken out of his hands. Yancey and his companion, alarmed by the ruckus, had forked it out.

Eyes peeled for trouble, he emerged from the surgery. The street was dimly lit from the lights spilling from buildings. Almost at once he recognized the lurking figure very near to the alleyway almost opposite. Casper! He'd been right. That no-good varmint had been waiting his chance to strike, but fortunately for Casper the Coyotes had ruined his plan. If it had not been for the Coyotes, Casper would have been gutted by now.

'Hell, Casper,' someone yelled. 'What the hell is going on?'

'How the hell do I know,' Casper rejoined. 'I was passed out back of the alley until all this ruckus woke me up?'

Rumble knew the varmint was lying. But what Casper had seen or had not seen was of little significance as far as Rumble was concerned.

Quickening his stride he headed east towards Mattie's place, and found Sheriff John Sloan had beaten him to it.

'Well, I reckon you've stomach enough for what's inside,' the lawman observed sourly. 'I ain't never encountered the like of this before and I don't reckon I will again.' He paused. 'There's two *hombres* inside, or what's left of them, for she has done chopped them into pieces, kept at it after they were dead, the whole damn parlour stinks of blood and gore.'

Entering the parlour Rumble saw what the lawman was talking about. Miz Mattie, he figured, must have been overcome by a killing frenzy. The woman herself a gruesome blood-soaked sight, seemed calm enough.

'Good evening, Doc Rumble.' She greeted him coolly. 'I'll be having a word with you tomorrow. Make sure you're available.'

'Hell, Miz Mattie, you ain't chopped Miz Broughton, have you?' the lawman questioned, sounding as though he wouldn't be surprised had she done so.

'Don't be absurd, Sheriff. Miz Broughton is safely in the bedroom. This is no sight for a young woman or child. They will stay in the bedroom until this mess is removed. Lord knows how I am going to clean up. But first the remains have to be removed.' She scarcely paused for breath. 'Those drunken bums wanted to murder us or worse. Two helpless women in their beds. Why else would they break into the home of respectable women?'

'But you weren't in bed! And you ain't even in your night attire.' The lawman took a deep breath. 'And you could have blasted them, Miz Mattie. Why take a chopper to them?' He shook his head, 'What do you think, Doc?'

Rumble knew better than to say what he thought. 'Most likely the bums were too drunk to know what they were doing. They made a mistake and paid the price. And as they ain't from Poynton no need to give yourself a headache trying to figure out why in tarnation they chose this particular window to break in through.'

'How do you know they ain't from Poynton,' Sloan queried.

'Just a hunch.'

'I'll get what's left of the varmints toted to the undertaker.' The sheriff squared his shoulders and eyed Miz Mattie. 'I can see you've plenty of cleaning to do. We'll talk in the morning.'

Outside the sheriff took a deep breath. 'I ain't never going to feel easy around that woman now I know what she is capable of.'

Rumble shrugged. 'Very likely those varmints would have snapped her neck or caved in her skull once they'd gotten what they came for.'

Sloan spat. 'Like you said, too drunk to know what they were about.' He glared at Rumble. 'I ain't a fool and maybe this had something to do with that boy you handed over to Mattie. But I ain't about to enquire into the matter. Like you said, they were drunken bums from out of town! And as for you, Doc Rumble, well I reckon the Devil looks after his own! And he sure as hell has looked after you. By the way I've received word that Epson will be heading West mighty soon. I'm expected to co-operate with the varmint. What do you say?'

'I say Epson is a proficient killer. No one Epson goes after stands trial and many don't die easy, so I've heard. He ain't a man to cross nor a man to help. Don't involve yourself in his plans. Death follows in his wake. Those who ride with him are expendable.' Rumble paused, 'And they ain't nothing but scum or they would not be riding with Epson!'

'But you'd cross him if he stood in your way. I can't fathom what brought you West, Doc Rumble, and now I am damn certain I do not wish to know. I wish you goodnight.'

As Yancey had expected there was no sound of pursuit. The two men had halted a safe distance from town.

'Hell! The boss is liable to blast us both the same way he did for Mince,' Nash griped. 'We've gotta get out of the territory pretty damn quick.'

'And give up our share of the loot coming our way? Are you loco? We both know the last job is gonna be one almighty haul. A fitting exit for the Coyotes.'

Nash was silent, then he said, much to Yancey's surprise, 'Well, we've gotta give the boss something to chew on. Something that ain't you and me, Yancey.'

'You mean someone,' Yancey corrected. 'The boss don't take to the crew thinking for themselves,' he continued. 'Kent don't take kindly to surprises. Who have you got in mind?'

'Those goddamn Mortimers! If the boss wants to know about the boy, well, I reckon he can ask the farmer a few questions. It will give him a chance to cool down, divert attention from us.' Nash looked straight at Yancey. 'Fact is, we've failed. Those no-account bums Fishwick and Clemence have messed up.'

'Yep.' Yancey spat. 'Seems like the woman got the better of them. Hell, whatever they got they deserved for letting that old girl best them.'

'What do you think happened to them?' Nash asked.

'Well, they didn't fork it out,' Yancey mused. 'So your guess is as good as mine. We'll collect the Mortimers on our way back. We can't predict how boss Kent is gonna react. It could make things worse for us. Or, like you say, having them around gives him a chance to cool down.' Both men knew the Mortimers would never leave the Lazy R alive.

'I'll give them a sporting chance,' Yancey declared. 'I'll toss a coin. Fate can decide whether you and me are gonna pay farmer Mortimer a visit. I can't say fairer than that. Are you agreed?'

'Yep.'

Yancey tossed the coin.

'I ain't leaving until I know what the hell is going on!' Miz Mattie declared. She'd cornered Rumble in his surgery.

'How was it you were waiting, axe to hand?' Rumble

queried. 'Was it me you were expecting to come through your window, Miz Mattie? If so, you don't know me at all.'

There was a long silence. 'I don't believe I want to know you, Doc Rumble. Now answer my question!'

'I believe you dispatched two members of the Coyotes last night.'

She didn't bat an eyelid but merely continued to glare at him.

'The Coyotes took Miss Lillian Thompson from the stage. Judge Thompson sent me West to get her back. Folk don't know Miss Thompson is missing. The judge has kept her locked away at home for many years, ever since Miss Thompson gave birth.'

'The boy. And this Judge Thompson wants the child?'

'Nope. Miss Lillian and her governess fooled the judge into thinking the child was dead and had been disposed of. No, it's Miss Lillian he wants back. It seems the girl is to inherit a tidy sum once she turns thirty provided she has remained of good character. But Miss Lillian got out and headed West in search of the child. The Coyotes got her before she was able to reach Poynton. Since then she's been seen riding with them. Judge Thompson has sent two others who have met with bad ends. I'm obliged to retrieve Miss Lillian and return her home without anyone being the wiser.'

He waited a moment, but Mis mattie made no comment. 'Captain Epson is heading West to deal with the Coyotes. If he gets hold of Miss Lillian she'll hang. I believe Epson particularly enjoys the sight of a female dangling at the end of a rope.'

'The mad dog!' Miz Mattie's eyes narrowed. 'So why are

you going along with Judge Thompson?'

Rumble sighed.

'I know when to keep my lips buttoned.' Mattie encouraged Rumble to respond.

'I have a sister. Rich folk took her in when Ma died. She's done well for herself; she's got an ambitious husband and a place in society. It wouldn't help if word got out she was kin to me!'

Mattie nodded. 'Well, you know you'll have to deal with Thompson. He'll double-cross you. Word will get out once Miss Lillian is safely home. Will this Miss Lillian still want her son?'

'Damned if I know,' he replied frankly. 'I have it on good authority that Miss Lillian Thompson is somewhat of a chameleon. She's liable to want him one day and not the next, so her old governess told me. Hell, Miz Mattie, I'm damned if I know how things are gonna end.'

She nodded. 'I can play a waiting game, Doc Rumble. As well as you, I'd say. But it's important not to wait too damn long. From where I'm standing it appears you've taken root in Poynton.' She sighed, 'I guess it depends on what those Coyotes aim to do next: and don't you be forgetting that varmint Frobisher. He will not have finished with you.'

'I ain't finished with him,' Rumble rejoined ominously. 'And how is Harriet Broughton?'

'Lord, she will not leave her bed. She has me waiting on her hand and foot.'

'No chance of her heading home to her pa?'

'I guess not, Doc Rumble. But if she stays with me she'll be safe enough Those damn Coyotes ain't finished with you and maybe not the boy. But I've a mind to blast anyone who comes calling without an invite.' The door slammed behind her. A moment later the sheriff entered.

'Hell! Those two dead galoots rode for a rancher answering to the handle of Kent. He runs a spread called the Lazy R in the vicinity of Upstanding. Higgins recognized their horses. I aim to ride out and have a word with the galoot myself,' Sloan stated, coming straight to the point. 'I'm gonna let him know two of his men came to Poynton intent on molesting respectable womenfolk. I want to know what he's got to say.'

'I'd advise against it.' Rumble's conscience chose this moment to surface. He felt obliged to warn the lawman. 'You've heard of the Coyotes, ain't you? If you do call in on Kent I'd advise you to tread carefully.'

There was a long silence. The lawman appeared to be thinking. 'I guess I'll leave them to you. That's why you're here, ain't it, Rumble? You been paid to deal with them.'

'I reckon,' Rumble agreed. But he did not elaborate.

'Your kind always attracts trouble,' the lawman observed.

'You've had your say. Now get. I'm gonna have a surgery full of griping folk to deal with. Trouble or not, they still knock on my door.'

Sloan took a deep breath. 'I'm telling you now, Rumble. When Epson hits Poynton I'm pointing him the direction of Richard Kent and the Lazy R. Those varmints deserve what's coming their way.'

'Hell, maybe I ought to have let you blunder into that hornet's nest. Now, like I said, I've sick folk to tend.'

'Do you reckon she's crazy?' Sloan asked on his way out.

'Some folk are saying she is. Miz Mattie has sure shook up this town.'

'Nope.' Rumble's thoughts turned to Miss Kathleen Clegg, Lillian Thompson's old governess. Judge Thompson sure had a lot to answer for.

CHAPTER 7

Doc Rumble stood outside his surgery. Across Main Street he spotted Miz Mattie and the boy headed for the general store. She sailed along, head held high, seemingly oblivious to the fact that folk were quick to get out of her way. Even Casper, no-account bum that he was, moved off the sidewalk when he saw her headed towards him.

Inside the store Mattie bought a slate, chalk and a stick of candy for her charge. The storekeeper practically stood to attention and wished her good morning with a bit too much cheer.

'Looks like we're going to have a mighty fine day, Miz Mattie,' he muttered uncomfortably as she paid for her purchases.

'I believe so.' She stared at him until he looked away.

'Looks like we're going to have a mighty fine day,' Richard Kent observed as he ushered the Mortimers on to his front porch. His crew were idling around in anticipation of the forthcoming show. His smile faded when he spotted one of the drunken bums his crew had gathered staggering towards the horse trough.

'That man, that man he looks like that monster Rumble!' Mrs Mortimer shrilled. 'Why, I would almost swear on the Good Book that it was he!'

'Well he ain't. If he was Mr Kent would see to it that the varmint got his just deserts,' Mortimer declared. He glowered at Kent, 'And what are you gonna do about the varmints who manhandled us, me and the wife, forcing us here while a courteous invite would have sufficed?'

'If you could delay your departure a moment, Mr Mortimer, I would be obliged. Miss Lillian wants to wish you farewell.'

As Mortimer grunted a wordless affirmative Kent saw that two of his crew were quickly ushering the bum back towards the bunkhouse reserved for the no-accounts. Protesting, the man was shoved inside. Kent beckoned and Yancey and Nash headed towards the porch.

'Damn varmints!' Mortimer spewed forth profanities as he saw the two approaching.

'I've got a task that even you two no-account useless bums ought to be able to manage!'

'Sure thing, boss.' Yancey knew what was coming. The Mortimers were in for one hell of an awakening. They were about to meet the real Richard Kent.

'You two varmints escort Mrs Mortimer to meet our other guests.'

'Sure thing.' Yancey and Nash took hold of Mrs Mortimer by each arm.

'What the hell!' Mortimer was clearly alarmed. His breath escaped in a gasp as Kent stomach-punched him and then followed with a kick to the ribs, as the farmer went down.

'Shut up and listen,' Kent snarled, all appearances of affableness vanishing. 'You see that horse yonder? Saddled and waiting? Well, that horse is your salvation. Reach that horse and you can ride out. Not one man here will try to stop you. Your good lady stays here. She can make herself useful.'

Howling, Mrs Mortimer was being forced into the bunkhouse. Yancey and Nash barred the door behind her, imprisoning her with the bums. Yancey chuckled. The bums had been griping that they had been promised women; well, now they were getting one!

Mortimer staggered to his feet. He clutched his stomach. He was more afraid now than he had ever been. He broke into a lolloping shamble. Pain shot through him. His wife was forgotten. All he could think about was saving himself.

Lillian Thompson came out on to the porch. She was smiling. She was also carrying a bow. At her back was a quiver of arrows. She needed to impress Richard Kent and Mortimer was expendable. Taking aim she brought him down, her first arrow hitting his leg. She fitted a second arrow. By the time she was finished Mortimer would doubtless resemble a porcupine. The luckless man, sobbing for mercy, was dragging himself towards the waiting horse. Lillian fired again. Mortimer twitched and screeched but kept crawling.

'Yancey!' Kent bellowed. Lillian's antics had only half his attention.

'You've seen the doc. Does the bum resemble him?'

'More or less. He's the bum collected by Clemence, but the fact is Clemence just picked up what he could get. He didn't go looking for a galoot with a likeness to himself. It turns out this one maybe could be mistaken for Rumble at a distance.'

From the bunkhouse housing the bums came a piercing scream. Kent smiled. Those goddamn bums would not be around to enjoy themselves for long.

The porcupine that was Mortimer stopped twitching.

Richard Kent rubbed his jaw. The ground was rock hard. 'Yancey,' he bellowed.

'Yes boss.'

'You and Nash can bury this no-account. And I want him buried deep. Six feet, no less!' Kent smiled. 'It will take a while. Get digging and think yourselves lucky I don't bury you two with him. Plant him deep then fill it in.'

A woman screamed.

Kent smiled,. 'Seems like those bums are amusing themselves.'

'Speaking of bums . . .' Yancey hesitated.

'Well!' Kent's good humour vanished.

'Seems like Tom Balding ain't back yet. We're a bum short.'

'There's yet time. At the moment we have no need to worry about Balding.'

But Kent knew this was not quite true. Balding should have returned. Balding was a loose end. For a moment Kent felt a *frisson* of unease that he could never admit to. He could never allow the men he led to doubt him, not for an instant. 'And dig a separate grave for the woman. We'll need to plant her sooner or later.'

Yancey nodded. Bending his bead to hide his sour expression he turned away. By the time he and Nash had finished digging their palms would be one hell of a mass of blisteas. But knowing Kent, he and Nash had gotten off lightly.

'I reckon the Coyotes have snatched the Mortimers,' Sheriff Sloan stated baldly. 'That's your doing.'

Rumble, much to the lawman's annoyance, did not reply. After some moments Sloan felt obliged to continue. 'I rode out this morning, meaning to have a word or two about the boy the Coyotes seemed so interested in. There were signs of a disturbance, a table laden with food overturned, smashed furniture and so on, which led me to believe they had not left of their own free will.'

Rumble shrugged. 'They ain't my concern. Nor should they be yours.'

'Damn it, Rumble, those Coyotes have got to be stopped. Hell! Epson can't get here soon enough for my liking'

Before Rumble could reply a volley of shots accompanied by loud whoops rang out. From the way Sloan jumped it was clear the lawman thought trouble in one form or another was hitting town. Cursing, Sloan hauled out his Peacemaker.

Rumble didn't move. The whooping was exuberant more than anything else. Clearly the Coyotes weren't paying Poynton a visit. He watched as the buggy careered down Main Street, causing folk to move out of the way with alacrity. It was the youngster sitting in the back of the buggy who was firing the shots and whooping with excitement.

'Hell! What do you mean by it?' Sloan bellowed as the buggy came to a jarring halt before the lawman.

'Dead men, Sheriff! Two of them,' the excited youngster yelled. 'Me and my brother found 'em.'

'I'll take a look,' Rumble stepped towards the buggy.

'No need for that, Doc. One of them has had the back of his head staved in and the other . . . well, seems like he just upped and died. We had a good look when we loaded them into the buggy.'

'You seen any riderless horses thereabouts?' the lawman questioned.

'We ain't looked.'

'You men get those men into my surgery.'

'What the hell for, Doc? They're dead,' an onlooker protested.

'You boys have been through their pockets, ain't you?' The lawman glared at the two farm boys.

'Naturally you can keep whatever cash you found.' Rumble stepped in. 'But hand over whatever else you took. We need to know who they are.'

'We ain't found nothing but this on the one that died natural.' The elder boy handed over a dog-eared family photograph.

'Turn out your pockets, you varmints. I don't take kindly to being lied to.'

Rumble watched as the boys turned out their pockets. Like they'd said, there was nothing else except a roll of bills.

'So what brought you to town?'

'Pa sent us in for supplies. We've been working real hard so Pa let us come in for the supplies.'

The lawman sighed. 'The supplies will have to wait. You

two boys are gonna show me exactly where you found these two galoots. I reckon it seems clear enough. They fell out and one staved in the head of the other. But no man ought to go to his grave without a name on his marker. We'll do right. A share of the money you found will go to pay the undertaker. The rest you can keep. We'll settle with him now.' He scowled; townsmen directed by Rumble were carrying the two dead men into the doctor's office.

'The undertaker can have them when I've finished with 'em,' Rumble declared. He closed the door of his surgery and the CLOSED sign went up.

Sloan thinned his lips. He had no time for the unpredictable loco doc. He was duty bound to swear in a posse and investigate the scene of the killing. He knew a lawman had to be seen to be earning his pay and this was as good a way as any.

Rumble had kept alive by paying attention to detail. And anything that happened around Poynton or thereabouts concerned him. He had a strong stomach and the stench of death did not concern him. Nor the fact that flies had been at the one whose head had been stoved in. There would be a hell of cleaning-up to do when he'd finished with these two. He got to work. Sometimes the dead could tell plenty if only someone thought to look.

Sometime later, when he'd finished with the two dead men and had seen them toted away to the town's undertaking establishment, Rumble headed for the livery barn. He needed to talk with Higgins.

'Hell, Doc, it ain't the same without her here,' Higgins grumbled as he sat down. at the table. 'I've got used to her telling me what to do and now there ain't no one around.'

'I ain't here to talk about Miz Mattie.'

'I didn't think you were.'

'I'm here to talk about this town and the Frobisher mine.'

'Well I ain't never been out there. You'll steer clear if you've any sense.'

'I've got a few questions and I reckon you can answer them.'

Rumble listened as Higgins answered his questions. But his thoughts were with the two dead galoots hauled into town. The two men had shared certain physical characteristics relating to face and build. The one whose head had been stoved in had seemed in good condition apart from the blow to the back of the head. He had looked to be nothing more than a waddy. The second, with his missing teeth and broken-vein features, had been a bum. He'd died from lack of water as he'd stumbled around in the fierce heat of the day. Rumble had opened up that one. The bum's liver was ruined. He hadn't troubled opening up the waddy. He'd simply guessed the man had liked his drink.

He'd taken a guess at what had happened. The two had sat round the campfire passing a bottle. The waddy had eventually keeled over but the bum being more accustomed to swilling down rotgut liquor had not keeled over. Instead the man had found a rock and stoved in the back of the waddy's head. But then it had gone sour. The stumbling bum hadn't been able to saddle up. The horses had got away, bolted no doubt, leaving the bum to stumble around until dehydration dispatched him to the hereafter.

The lawman was returning with two riderless horses. Rumble rose to his feet. His hunch was correct. One of the horses carried the Lazy R brand. For a reason as yet unknown the boss of the Coyotes was collecting bums: men who would not be missed.

Rumble tried to put himself in Richard Kent's boots. What would he do if he were running the Coyotes? Sure as hell he would know it would all have to come to an end one way or another. A wise man would be making plans to quit the territory and disappear. And maybe Kent was planning to do just that!

It was glaringly obvious that the bums were expendable. They would not be missed. Kent had not brought the bums together without good reason.

'Hold up a moment, Sherif.' The telegraph clerk came bounding along the street, clearly excited by the news he was bringing. 'I've just received word from Captain Epson. He plans to be in Poynton pretty soon. He says to make yourself available.' The man was all agog. 'I reckon those damn Coyotes are gonna get their just deserts mighty soon.'

'Give me that damn telegraph.' The lawman snatched the missive. 'And get about your business.'

'What do you say, Doc?' The clerk was inclined to tarry.

Rumble smiled coldly. 'I'm in favour of folk getting their just deserts!' As long as it wasn't himself! If he'd been given his just deserts he would have been planted way back. As it was he'd continued to prosper and saw no reason for things to change. He aimed to get back to city life pretty damn quick but first there were certain matters to be taken care of.

'Well, I reckon Kent will be running scared pretty soon,' the lawman observed once the pesky clerk had retreated.

At first Rumble did not reply; surely it had to be clear that Kent was not a man to run scared. Richard Kent was a devious, merciless varmint and right now Kent was hatching plans. 'I'm headed out,' he announced, coming to an inevitable decision. 'If I don't come back assume I'm dead meat.'

The lawman shrugged. 'I won't try to dissuade you. I guess you know your own mind.'

After picking up supplies at the general store Rumble headed for the livery barn. He could not help noticing Higgins looked mighty relieved once he'd realized the only thing he was required to do was saddle a horse. Nor did Higgins enquire as to where the doc might be headed. Rumble was not troubled. For as long as he could remember he'd relied on himself. He'd always been able to see to his own survival. He'd never sink as low as that varmint Richard Kent and right now Rumble was convinced the boss of the Coyotes was also preoccupied with survival.

Yancey stroked his chin. He'd never been able to figure out how it was his boss Richard Kent, a fastidious gentleman, had become acquainted with the stinking varmint known hereabouts, on account of his round bland features, as Moonface. Yancey scratched himself vigorously. He'd just bought a supply of lice killer from the peddler. He wondered why Moonface didn't avail himself of his own products. Even as boss Kent was speaking

Moonface was scratching vigorously. Yancey was not fooled by the man's wide grin and simple manner. The peddler was a wolf in sheep's clothing. Yancey could not hear what was being said but Moonface was beaming wider than ever as he nodded enthusiastically.

'I have a task for you, Yancey.' Kent strolled over to the waddy once Moonface had driven away. 'You're to see to it immediately. And this time if you mess up I will have your hide. I've made allowance for you once but your luck done run out.' Succinctly he gave his instructions.

'But can the varmint be trusted?' Yancey enquired.

'Sure he can, as much as any man.' Kent smirked, 'Moonface is a snake. But snakes can have their uses.'

Yancey turned away stifling a smirk of his own. They were all goddamn snakes and that was a fact. As he headed for the bunkhouse housing the bums, he wondered what plans Doc Rumble was hatching.

The peddler Moonface drove into the Frobisher mine without being challenged.

'Got any lice killer?' a guard yelled.

'I sure have.' Moonface grinned. 'And I have a remedy for gut-gripe, brewed by myself so I know it works.'

Frobisher tolerated him. The sight of his wagon from time to time kept the bored guards happy. 'I've a few of my special prints ordered from back East.' His special prints of scantily clad females were always much in demand and fetched a high price. 'And after I have served you gentlemen perhaps one of you could enquire whether Mr Frobisher will grant me a few moments of his time? I have something to say which will interest him greatly.' He knew better than to barge in and disturb Norman Frobisher, for the man, like Richard Kent, had been given an unpleasant disposition. He was capable of first offering a man a brew of coffee and then cutting his throat.

While Moonface peddled his wares Norman Frobisher, alone in the cabin that was his office and home, prayed. His 'slave' workers were not worth a spit. Another one had died this morning. Some were brought to his mine by force, others were reeled in by promises of good pay for hard work. None of them left until it was time to be planted. And as for the guards, he employed only a certain type of man: men without conscience. He knew some had sniggered privately about how the cursed doctor had dealt with Morgan with seeming ease. Frobisher prayed that Doc Rumble would be delivered into his hands. He would not be able to walk tall until the man who had defied his authority was dead.

It had been a stinking old galoot with round, moonfaced features who had given Rumble the journal by way of payment.

'I ain't troubled reading it myself.' The fellow had kept grinning as he had held out the dirt-begrimed journal. Rumble had thanked the man. There was just something about the galoot that had made his flesh crawl.

'*The Journal of an English Gentleman in the West,*' he had read. He did not enquire as to how his 'patient' had come by the journal. He had read the journal. The English gentleman had certainly explored the terrain hereabouts before the journal had fallen into the hands of the old varmint.

Rumble had determined that if this English gentleman

had been able to find his way to High Ridge then he himself could do no less. The instructions were precise. With the aid of a compass Rumble proceeded slowly. He heaved a sigh of relief when the towering outline of the mountain ridge came into sight. Jagged and threatening was how some might describe High Ridge. Others might describe it as majestic. Rumble was not given to such pondering. To him High Ridge was neither jagged and threatening nor majestic. It was merely a mountain that was not as inaccessible as folk hereabouts seemed to think.

Upon reaching the base of High Ridge, Rumble consulted the journal. The English gentleman was mighty fine when it came to sketching. Rumble was prepared to gamble that the sketch was accurate enough. He dismounted and led his horse. It would never be able to outrun if pursuit were given but its damn slowness was what had appealed to Rumble. As yet he was not much of a horseman and he was damned proud of himself for managing to ride out and find High Ridge.

'Where are we headed,' the bum who bore a striking resemble to Doc Rumble whined. He'd been cleaned up and respectably suited; the suit bore a similarity to the garb favoured by Rumble.

'You and me, we're gonna share a jug,' Yancey slurred. 'The further away from that no- account boss of mine the better.'

'He ain't so bad.' the bum, who answered to the name of Bill, seemed inclined to defend the boss of the Lazy R.

Yancey chuckled. Richard Kent was mighty good at fooling folk when it suited his purpose. 'We'll share a jug.

Have a snooze then head back. Hell, ain't none of those varmints going to miss us two.'

'Hell no,' the bum agreed, puzzled by the turn of events but unable to think beyond the jug.

Rumble found the opening in the rock face. Just as the English gentleman had done Rumble managed to get a bandanna over his horse's eyes. Then he led the animal through the narrow passageway. He cut stunted scrub and concealed the entrance way behind him. As described, the rock face loomed before him, water trickling down to pool in a shallow indentation.

Leaving his horse untethered Rumble began the climb that, according to the English gentleman, would lead him up to the narrow ridge itself. And from that ridge he would be able to look down upon the Frobisher mine and the surrounding terrain.

'Hell, Higgins, where's that critter you promised me,' the proprietor of Poynton's eating-house demanded.

'Fact is I sold it,' Higgins answered reluctantly.

'What fool would buy that critter? It's run out of time. All it's good for is my slow-cooked stew.'

'It's gone, and as to who bought it, well, that ain't none of your damn business,' Higgins snapped. No way would he ever divulge that Doc Rumble had seemed mighty impressed with the animal. And the doc had offered far more than the restaurant proprietor. Higgins shook his head. He'd warned the doc the animal was no damn use. Like Higgins himself, it had seen better days.

CHAPTER 8

'I guess you've seen better days,' Yancey observed as he passed the jug to the eager bum. Whereas Yancey had taken care merely to sip the rotgut liquor, his companion had gulped down as much as he could without choking himself.

The man grunted an unintelligible reply as he grabbed the jug. With shaking hands he raised it to his lips.

'Well, I reckon it's time.' Yancey spoke to himself. Sure as hell the worthless bum was incapable of understanding a word. In Yancey's opinion the bum, deliberately drinking himself insensible with no thought of anything other than rotgut liquor, could not blame anyone other than himself for the way the cards fell.

Yancey's hand closed over the small but heavy hammer he had placed in his jacket pocket.

This would be so easy; the bum – Bill he'd called himself – was gulping down the liquor, his eyes shut like a baby at its bottle. Yancey raised a wiry arm and brought it down hard. His target was Bill's kneecap. As the hammer head smashed against Bill's knee, bone shattered. Helpless beneath the ferocious onslaught, Bill screamed a terrible sound that did not affect his assailant one bit. The jug went flying, its contents spilling and seeping into the hard ground.

'Ain't nothing personal, Bill.' Yancey grinned. 'It's just your misfortune to bear a resemblance to a certain Doctor Dennis Rumble.'

Bill, howling in agony, had rolled into a ball. As expected, Bill had not tried to defend himself, and for that Yancey felt only contempt.

Yancey retrieved the jug and downed the few dregs that had not seeped away. He wiped his mouth, then, taking both horses, headed back in the direction of the Lazy R confident that the crippled man would not even try to move away from where he had been left.

Yancey found himself thinking about the genuine article: the real Dennis Rumble. He had the most uncomfortable feeling that if Rumble were not taken care of there would be no safety for any of them.

Sweat still trickled down Rumble's face. His shirt stuck to his back! Hell, he'd been obliged to get down on his hands and knees, forced to crawl along the spine of High Ridge, sheer drop on either side of him. And on the way to the summit he'd been beset by hordes of black flies who'd been in danger of flying into his mouth should he be so unwise as to unclamp his teeth. Leastways up here, where the air was a mite cooler they had been left behind.

Now he was settled in a shallow basin at the top of High Ridge where the ridge had temporarily widened. Stunted shrubs dotted the basin. This was the vantage point from where the English gentleman had observed the wilderness below, a wilderness marred by a sprawling mine, the fellow had written.

Right now Rumble's gaze was fixed in the opposite direction to the mine. A spyglass was pressed against his eye. He'd been able to recognize the minute spots below, the two men who had settled against a fallen tree to pass the jug. One was Yancey and the other, Rumble felt compelled to concede, bore a striking resemblance to himself. He'd watched as Yancey had attacked the other, smashing a hammer again and again against the look-alike's knee. And now that varmint Yancey was riding away, leaving the other man crippled and helpless.

Well, there was nothing to be done for the man. Rumble turned away and, moving to the other side of the shallow basin, focused his attention on the Frobisher mine. A wagon was just driving through the heavily guarded mine entrance.

Rumble had begun to suspect that Richard Kent and the Coyotes intended to raid the mine, a haul that would make the rest of their loot seem as nothing in comparison.

He had also began to suspect that Epson had to be involved in this set up. It had to be so because Richard Kent would find it an impossibility to throw Epson off his trail. The man would arrive with a veritable army at his disposal. The unfortunate drunks whom Kent's men had collected together were going to serve as decoys. There wasn't any other use for them that Rumble could think of.

He did not need to understand why Epson was involved. Nor was he curious to know why the hitherto incorruptible Captain Epson had turned crooked, throwing in his lot with the outlaw band he'd been hired to exterminate.

'Stay put. You keep away from me. Do you hear?' Frobisher glared at the old man, ill pleased that his prayers had been disturbed. 'You stink like rotten cabbage!'

Moonface just kept grinning. 'I heard tell you're aching to get your hands on a certain galoot,' he essayed.

'What the hell do you mean?' Frobisher toyed with a glass paperweight. He felt tempted to hurl it at the man's round smiling face.

'Folk gossip. I hear things. And sometimes I see things.'

Frobisher picked up the paperweight. His patience evaporated. 'Spit it out or get out of my sight.' Hell, he was gonna hurl the paperweight. And with a bit of luck the blow might kill the godddamn peddler. Of course the men would grumble about not being able to get their hands on the racy prints the man peddled but Frobishier didn't give a damn.

The peddler spoke quickly, noticing the way Frobisher's hand had closed over the paperweight. 'Doc Rumble,' he grunted and, as he had hoped, the sound of the hated name caused Frobisher to carefully replace the paperweight. 'It's Yancey. That damn fool doc paid Yancey to guide him out so as he could get a closer look at the mine. Now there ain't no call for alarm,' he soothed as Frobisher cursed.

'You damn fool,' Frobisher yelled.

'Naturally Yancey double-crossed the doc,' Moonface continued, wisely ignoring the interruption. 'He done

crippled the doc and left him in the wilderness to die.'
The peddler grinned maliciously. 'I reckon my good
tidings deserve a coin or two,' he cajoled.

'You damn dog!' Frobisher hurled a couple of coins
down in the dirt for the filthy old peddler to scrabble for.
On his way out of the cabin he planted his boot on
Moonface's backside, sending the man to sprawl face
down in the dirt.

Moonface bit back the foul curse that came naturally to
his lips. Frobisher was a damn fool. And he wouldn't be
around much longer.

'Where the hell is he?' The mine boss saw he still hadn't
wiped the smile from the peddler's face. 'Where the hell
can I find Dennis Rumble?'

'Can I ride along with you? I'd like to see the fun.' The
peddler smirked after giving directions.

'You stinking old varmint, you are enough to turn any
man's stomach. One of these days I'm going to wipe that
grin off your face. Get off my property. I don't want to see
you back here for a very long time!'

'You can count on that,' the peddler muttered. But
Frobisher wasn't listening. The mine boss was yelling for
his crew to saddle up.

As Richard Kent had predicted, Frobisher would not
ride out alone. He would suspect a trap. And Frobisher
was right. A trap was being sprung, but not the kind
Frobisher imagined.

'If you ain't played straight I'll have your guts,'
Frobisher yelled as he rode from the mine. 'Don't think I
won't hunt you down.'

Moonface kept on smiling. He was counting on being

hunted down. He began to whistle as he drove away from the mine. There were plenty of gullies and plenty of scrubland. The terrain provided good places to hide out. Not that anyone ever escaped from the mine. Frobisher's slave workers kept right on shovelling until they dropped dead.

He glanced at his pocket watch. By now Yancey would have reported back to Richard Kent. Moonface smiled. He and Richard went way back. It had been he who had taught the boss of the Lazy R all he knew. Nobody knew it, but Richard Kent was the peddler's grandson.

Richard Kent lit a cigar. 'For a moment I wondered whether the bum had got the better of you.' He eyed Yancey coldly, pleased to see that Yancey couldn't decide whether the words were a joke or a warning.

'Damn shame you were forced to use a substitute, boss,' one of the crew observed maliciously.

Yancey knew the remark was directed at himself and Nash. He did not react.

'You there, Riley.' Kent glared at the man who had spoken up. 'Do you think you can get the bums out and sobered up without alarming then?'

'Sure thing, boss.' Riley was eager to oblige.

'I reckon it's time those varmints paid for their keep,' Kent continued, thinking that Riley was on the way to becoming a drunkard himself. 'Yancey, get inside and brew a plentiful supply of coffee. Those varmints need to be able to ride. You go with Riley to the line cabin. Feed and bed them down. As far as they are concerned they're to start rounding up my strays mighty soon.'

'Sure thing, boss!'

Riley peered into the bunkhouse housing the bums. As the stench from within hit him he stepped backwards.

'Time to get to work, you varmints,' he nevertheless yelled cheerfully, 'Out you come. Dip your heads in the trough then set yourselves down for coffee and biscuits. You're heading out once you've sobered up. It's time to earn your keep rounding up the boss's strays. This ranch ain't a guest house and that's a fact. We all work around here.'

'We sure do,' Nash agreed with a grin. Did those damn no-accounts really think they would be any use to the boss?

'Just look at that.' Riley, the Irishman, laughed as the no-good drunks enthusiastically dipped their heads into the water trough. One had come up with the idea and the others had followed suit.

'I know you men won't let me down,' Richard Kent encouraged. 'You men are gonna prove those who said you weren't worth a spit damn wrong. I know good men when I see them!' He also recognized gullible fools. 'Yancey, you no-account varmint, fetch these men their coffee. And be quick about it. They ain't got all day!'

Riley, who had gone into the bunkhouse, peered down at Mrs Mortimer. His victuals threatened to come up. One of the varmints having lost control, had smashed her head to pulp. But then, nobody had expected her to leave the bunkhouse alive. Her grave, freshly dug, was waiting. Like the no-account bums she would not be missed.

'Get that woman planted while the bums sober up,' Kent ordered from the bunkhouse door.

'Sure thing, boss.'

Kent stuck a cigar between his lips. He glanced at his watch. By now Frobisher would have found Rumble's double. He had to take his hat off to Lilly, for it had been she who'd planted at letter written by herself in the double's wallet.

He strode towards his horse yelling for his crew, his Coyotes, to mount up. They had all been given their instructions. The slave workers weren't worth a spit nor a bullet, but everyone else left behind to guard the mine workings was to be blasted, save one. Kent thinned his lips. In this venture timing was everything. He was not entirely convinced that all would go according to plan. But then he'd always been a gambling man!

From High Ridge, Rumble watched as Norman Frobisher and most of his men rode out. The fool had left the mine almost unguarded. And with the Coyotes around that was not a wise move. The peddler had clearly told Frobisher where he'd be able to find Doc Rumble and the mine boss had taken the bait.

Rumble had to accept that he could not save his double from whatever vengeance Frobisher intended dishing out. He could not reach the man in time. And even if this had been possible it would have been a hopeless task.

All he could do was watch from his high vantage point. Using his spyglass he had a bird's-eye view. In one direction lay the mine. In another the man who was almost his double lay slumped against a fallen tree. He knew it was too much to hope that Frobisher would be inclined to show this man mercy. Frobisher would want to send a message. He would want to tell folk loud and clear to keep their noses out of what went on at his mine.

Richard Kent, knowing the kind of man Frobisher was, had used Frobisher's craving for vengeance for his own purpose. He'd seen a way to lure Frobisher and his guards away from the mine and he had taken it. Kent and his Coyotes were going to rob the mine whilst Frobisher was engaged elsewhere. And Epson had to be part of the plot.

It all made sense now, the way Kent had collected bums: stand-ins for himself and his crew. Men Epson could dispose of. Epson was too damn smart to have the wool pulled over his eyes. For the plan to work Epson had to be a party to it all. Rumble guessed that right now Epson was in Poynton; the bounty hunter was in place to hunt down and destroy the men deemed to be the Coyotes.

Rumble cursed softly. Frobisher had reached the luckless double. And of course, not knowing what was going on the man would think he was to be rescued. Rumble knew he would need a strong stomach for what he was about to witness. He had never felt as helpless as he did now. For once in his life he had done right and now another was about to suffer in his stead. He felt guilt because of this, a new emotion for him, but at the same time he was mighty glad that it was not he who had fallen into Frobisher's clutches.

Leading his crew of legally sanctioned cut-throats into Poynton, Captain Epson was glad to see he was causing a stir. He liked nothing better than to ride into a two-bit town at the head of his men. He liked seeing fear and awe on the faces turned his way. The feelings of pleasure he got from being recognized as a man of importance had never lessened over the time he had been bringing wrongdoers to justice.

'Get on down to the livery barn,' he ordered his men. 'I'll join you shortly.' With disgust he found himself staring at the freshly painted shingle that proclaimed the name of the town's doctor, one Dennis Rumble.

The tall lawman lounging against a hitching rail on the opposite side of Main Street made no move to cross over and speak with Epson, thus obliging Epson to be the one to make the first approach.

'You've got a no-account killer working in your town,' Epson warned.

The lawman did not react as expected. He shrugged. 'Don't concern yourself, Captain Epson. Thanks to Miss Broughton folk in Poynton know all about Doc Rumble. Leastways he don't kill his patients as our last doc did. This one won't touch liquor. He's a popular man.'

'Goddamnit man. You ought to have run that varmint out of town,' Epson rejoined.

'The frontier is a place for killers,' the lawman observed softly. He smiled unpleasantly. 'So I reckon neither one of you is out of place on the frontier. That's what you do, ain't it Epson? Shoot the men you hunt down like dogs?'

'The scum I go after don't deserve to live.'

'I'm Sheriff John Sloan by the way.' The lawman introduced himself. 'And before you ask I won't be riding with you when you go after the Coyotes. You ain't my kind of lawman, Captain Epson, and that is a fact.'

Epson spat. 'I didn't figure anyone in this two-bit town had the stomach to go after the Coyotes. This is man's work.' Sloan, he was annoyed to see, did not react to the insult. But before he could goad the lawman further Epson spotted Harriet Broughton, newspaper proprietor's daughter, staring his way and clearly getting ready to make himself the subject of her fool gossip.

Suddenly incensed, Epson spurred his horse forward and confronted her. 'What the hell are you gossiping about, you. . . ?'

Harriet Broughton taking a step backwards tumbled over and showed a good deal of ankle before she scrambled to her feet.

'That's enough. I'll have no trouble in my town. In my town respectable women are treated with respect.' Sheriff Sloan now held a sawn-off shotgun in his hands and the gun was pointed directly Epson.

'You want to watch what you say, Miss Broughton,' Epson advised. 'Or one day you're liable to disappear the way a certain Judge Thompson has disappeared. And before you ask if the judge's disappearance was my doing, the answer is no. I don't give a damn about Judge Thompson. Now I'll wish you good day, ma'am. I have work to do.'

'What was all that about, Miss Broughton?' the lawman asked as the bounty hunter rode towards the livery barn.

'I'm sure I cannot say, Sheriff. Now if you will excuse me.' Harriet Broughton hurried away. Thankfully she had not yet told any tales relating to the many ways Epson had been snubbed by his betters, for Captain Epson had always failed to realize that he could never be accepted as an equal.

At the livery barn Epson delivered his usual speech to the men. 'I'll blast any one of you who cannot sit a horse when it's time to ride out,' he threatened. 'I'll not have drunken bums in my crew. When it comes to the shootout each and every one of you is expected to be capable of hauling iron and shooting straight. While you're in Poynton you keep out of trouble. There will be no ruckus in this town. Do you understand me?'

'Sure thing, boss,' the men mumbled, knowing a response was expected.

'You there, ostler. See to the horses!' Epson bellowed.

Higgins, who had been about to ask the captain how long the hunting party intended staying in town, thought better of it. Wisely he kept his lips buttoned.

'There he is boss,' a voice yelled. But Frobisher had already seen the slumped figure. And the man, upon seeing them, hauled himself upright with an unintelligible grunt before collapsing again.

There was nowhere for anyone to hide. No rocks for men to shoot from as they sprung an ambush. Frobisher had been primed for a trap. But it was as that no-account skunk Moonface had said: Doc Rumble had been crippled and left to die a lingering death.

To the right of Frobisher Edwards, who had been with Joe Morgan when the doc had confronted them, clamped his lips shut. He'd been about to josh that they all looked damn foolish bristling with hardware just to take care of one galoot but he now thought better of it, for Frobisher was a mean-hearted unpredictable varmint.

'Something funny, Edwards?' Frobisher snarled.

'Just having a laugh at the doc's expense,' Edwards replied easily. 'He sure looks a sorry sight.'

113

'You were with Joe Morgan!' Frobisher glared at his hired man.

Edwards nodded, the amusement fading from his expression.

'And this man is Dennis Rumble?'

'Well, I reckon,' Edwards replied carefully.

'Get down. Go through his pockets,' Frobisher ordered curtly. 'For it seems to me you don't sound so sure.'

Edwards, wiping his brow, approached the doc. Roughly he rifled through the helpless, barely conscious man's pockets. He withdraw a faded wallet which contained one or two bills and a folded letter. Without a word he handed his find to his boss.

Frobisher unfolded the letter. It was undated. And it was from a woman thanking the doctor for his help and inviting him to call round if there was anything he needed. 'From a grateful widow' she had signed herself below a single initial. It was all the proof Frobisher needed.

'He's gonna look a damn sight sorrier before he's done.' Frobisher speculatively eyed the dead trunk of the fallen tree against which Doc Rumble slumped. 'Damn fool!' he concluded.

CHAPTER 9

Once Frobisher had ridden out the handful of men he had left behind to guard the place immediately took advantage of his absence. And why not? For when he was there they worked from dawn to dusk. They drew straws to see which two were to remain below ground overseeing the forced labour. That settled, the rest set up a table before one of the cabins; finding themselves a pack of cards and a jug of liquor they took advantage of Frobisher's absence.

One of their number who was not of a mind for cards amused himself regarding the scandalous prints of barely dressed females recently purchased from the peddler.

'Hell,' he grumbled, 'these women are a damn sight more appealing than the real ones I get my hands on.'

'You've said it,' another agreed. 'And ain't none of these women ever going to head West, and if they did ain't no way any would show their nose near this stink hole.'

Ribald remarks and loud hoots followed this observation, only ceasing when two riders were observed slowly approaching the mine entrance. At that the men came to their feet and readied themselves for trouble.

Then one of them laughed. 'There's no call for alarm. They ain't owl hoots. Fact is I recognize one of them. He's Richard Kent, boss of the Lazy R ranch, our nearest neighbour. The other must be one of his crew.'

'Hell! What do they want here?' The questioner carefully put his prints into his vest pocket 'Damnation, why can't it be good-looking women riding in?' he grumbled.

'No way good-looking women would be interested in you,' a companion joshed. The rifles that had been taken up had now been set down to lean against the card-table.

'The boss ain't around right now. Are you prepared to wait?' the guard in charge of the group asked grudgingly. 'Or shall I relay a message?'

Kent smiled. He did not seem put out by the news that Frobisher was absent. 'A message will suffice,' he replied. The smile did not quite reach his eyes. 'How many of you are there? It seems to me your boss has left you men thin on the ground,' he essayed.

'Well, there are the five of us you can see, and there are two below ground keeping an eye on those lazy—'

'What boss Frobisher does is his business,' the head guard cut in curtly, glaring at the fool who had started gabbing. 'Now I'd be obliged if you'd relay your message. There ain't none of us got the time to stand around gabbing.'

'I understand.' Kent nodded. 'And the fact is we have an urgent matter to take care of ourselves. Ain't that so, Nash?'

'Sure is, boss,' Nash agreed. At that both men simultaneously levelled their rifles and blasted away. As

116

previously agreed Frobisher took care of the three to the right, Nash dealt with the two standing slightly to the left of himself and his boss. As the boss had said, it was no more difficult than blasting sitting ducks.

An awareness of a glint of light from the corner of his right eye caused Nash to turn his head. He stared up at the towering high ridge, the spine of a mountain range running a considerable distance. There was nothing to see. And hell, he knew damn well it was impossible for anyone to be upon High Ridge, no horse could make it up top even if there had been a trail leading up there.

Nash stared down at the five dead bodies. He kept his lips buttoned, for boss Kent had clearly noticed nothing amiss.

'Damn fools,' Kent declared staring down at the dead men. 'Nash, keep a look out for the two below. Try to keep them pinned down if they show their faces. Remember I don't want them killed.' He was counting on at least one of the two having sense enough to fork it out and raise the alarm. But, he reflected as his own men rode in, there was no greater fool than Norman Frobisher.

'Lucky for you,' Frobisher addressed the miserable wretch he believed to be Rumble, 'lucky for you I can't spare the time to give you the send off you deserve, you meddling no-account varmint.'

It was true. He had left the mine undermanned and although he'd gamble all would be well enough he recognized it was wise to get back pretty damn quick.

'Get him roped to that old tree,' Frobisher ordered. 'I know just the way to deal with this meddlesome galoot!

And make sure "my friend" here can't part company from the wood.' He laughed, 'That wouldn't do. Not at all.'

'Hell, boss why not put a bullet in his head and be done with it,' a disgruntled voice queried.

Frobisher glared at the man who'd questioned his orders, and felt a desire to smash a fist into the fellow's face. Instead he forced himself to explain the obvious. 'We can't have folk sticking their noses into what goes on at the mine. Next thing we know I'll have reformers intent on putting the world to rights turning up at the workings demanding we let our workers feel free to leave if they want. If we ain't got workers able to work from dawn to dusk profits go down, when profits go down your bonuses go down. . . .'

'Not to mention your share of the profits, Mr Frobisher!'

The mine boss nodded. 'You've got the picture. So we must make an example of the doc. That way no one else from Poynton will meddle in mine business.'

'There ain't no one in Poynton interested anyway?'

'And we want to make sure things don't change. Get on with it. It's got to be done.' To his surprise no one made a move. 'I'll attend to the matter myself, then.' Dismounting, he approached the tied man and sloshed keroscene over both man and tree.

His intended victim, realizing what was about to happen, began to shriek. high-pitched sounds of pure terror. Frobisher, ignoring the screams, set light to the kindling. At first the small flicker of flame looked in danger of dying but then it began to take hold.

Mesmerized Frobisher and his men watched as the

ghastly scene unfolded. Not one of them made a move to grant the writhing man the mercy of a bullet. The screams reached a crescendo and Edwards broke. He put a bullet into the twitching burnt thing that was Dennis Rumble. The smell of burnt meat filled the air and men began to turn away from each other.

'Damnation!' a man exclaimed. 'That's the kind of thing those no-account Coyotes get up to.'

Frobisher turned towards the man who had fired the shot but Edwards stood his ground.

'Seems to me, Mr Frobisher,' he declared, 'seems to me Moonface ain't a man to do a favour for one or two miserly dollars. Hell, that peddler would take great delight in seeing your desire for vengeance thwarted, for that's the kind of twisted galoot he is. No, Moonface didn't tell you about Rumble's plight so that be could earn himself a dollar or two. I reckon there's more to this than meets the eye. Dennis Rumble has been used as a decoy. You can fire me if I am wrong.'

'You can count on that.' Frobisher swung into the saddle, uncomfortably aware that the words rang true. 'Let's ride.' Viciously he jabbed his horse with silver-starred spurs. Edwards would be paid off but not right now, for maybe he was damn right. There was something going on here and the peddler, a man he had always assumed to be a simpleton, had to be in on it.

They rode with reckless speed. A double-cross made sense. The peddler had been zigzagging the territory, peddling his wares, and in all that time the Coyotes had never troubled the man. And this could not be because Moonface was damn lucky.

Sickened, Rumble had turned away as his luckless double had been set on fire. He himself was safe enough, up high with his bird's-eye view of what was going on below. He swung round and placing his spyglass to an eye regarded the mine. As he'd expected a hold-up was in progress. He was in time to see the five men fall, three taken down by the tall impressive man who just had to be Richard Kent, boss of the Lazy R.

Kent had a familiar look about him but Rumble knew he had not encountered the man previously. But then, when the shorter, squatter man's head turned to tilt up as the galoot eyed High Ridge, Rumble dropped his spyglass with a curse, afraid the glint of light upon glass might have betrayed his presence. But what if it had? There was no way any of them could reach him up here. Men scrambling along a perilous path hardly wide enough to walk along were sitting ducks. He was perfectly safe.

Just as long as you stay up here! The thought sprang unbidden into his mind. He was aware that it was impossible to remain as an eye in the sky. Sooner rather than later he would be obliged to make the descent.

He did not need to be watching the layout below to know what was going to happen. Mighty soon Frobisher and his band of no-accounts would be back. They'd give pursuit, hell-bent on vengeance. Maddened with fury Frobisher would think of nothing other than getting back the stolen gold. He would not hesitate to take on the Coyotes.

Natusally, Richard Kent would realize this. Rumble was

pretty sure Kent wanted Frobisher to give pursuit. He'd be counting on it and would have hatched plans accordingly. Clearly the Coyotes, who would only be one step ahead, would not be safe until the mine boss and his crew were out of the picture.

Rumble knew that this was going to be a time for killing. It had already started. An innocent man had been burnt alive upon a whim. And mighty soon he would have to shrug off his reluctance and involve himself. He'd come West to take Miss Lillian Thompson back to her pa and that was what he was going to do. But he knew himself to be at a disadvantage. He was not at his best on the frontier. He was a city man, at home on mean streets and dark alleys. This wilderness was not his forte. And if he did not tread carefully very likely he would get himself killed. And from what he'd seen, from what he knew of the mine boss and the boss of the Coyotes, neither would be disposed to give him a quick ending by way of a merciful bullet.

Instead of moving he seated himself as comfortably as possible and once again began to peruse the worn journal the peddler Moonface had given him in lieu of payment.

'I ain't read it myself,' the man bad admitted, 'but the sketches are mighty fine.'

And so they were, Rumble agreed. The English gentleman had sketched animals and plants as well as the landscape. Small cramped writing filled each page. Significantly faded stains of what Rumble took to be dried blood marred the pages, for whoever had flicked through the journal had done so with bloodstained fingers. And without doubt those fingers had belonged to the murderously inclined old peddler.

'Hell!' On the last page the fool of an English gentleman had written of seeing an approaching wagon. And in anticipation of company the fool had put coffee to brew. For the Western man likes his coffee the idiot had concluded.

'Yep, and certain varmints like nothing better than robbing and killing,' Rumble muttered realizing that that damn fool of an English gentleman had paid for his carelessness with his life. And Moonface himself, unable to read, had failed to realize there was more to the journal than mighty fine sketches.

Rumble closed the journal. He'd found what he needed to know.

At the mine two men emerged from the fetid darkness of the tunnels. A volley of shots drove them back.

Garvey, the smarter of the two, yelled to his companion to keep back. 'Let them have the goddamn gold,' Garvey yelled. 'If the boss wants it back he can go after them himself. I tell you, White, I have a bad feeling about this business.'

'Do you reckon they'll come in after us?' White enquired nervously.

'Nope.' Garvey was emphatic. 'We know these tunnels like the backs of our hands. If they are fool enough to try and winkle us out they are done for. They know it. And they ain't interested in us.'

'They're riding out.' White sighed with relief. His gun hand was shaking. Garvey gripped his companion's arm. 'Let's make sure they are.' Some time later both men cautiously emerged.

Garvey scarcely heard a word White gabbled, for he was a man who always followed his hunches and he had a hunch that right now this mine was not the best place to be. He was damn sure the boss would unjustly blame himself and White for not stopping the robbery.

'I'm headed into town. The law has got to be told.'

'Boss Frobisher will be back any time now,' White gabbled. 'Hell, the boss will want to keep a lid on this. He won't want the law involved. He won't want word to spread that no-accounts have ridden in here and helped themselves.'

Ignoring the five dead men Garvey saddled his horse. 'Quit trying to put yourself in another man's boots,' he advised. 'I'm headed into Poynton. Ride with me. It will be better if you do.'

White hesitated. He shook his head. 'Nope. I owe it to the boss to stay around and discourage any of our workers from making a break for it.'

'Suit yourself, you damn idiot.' Garvey rode out. He would indeed head for Poynton if only to pick up supplies. After that he would keep right on riding. He was through with Frobisher. He knew the man would never accept that the blame lay on his own shoulders.

Epson took a corner table at the saloon. He waved away the saloon women who approached him offering comfort by the hour. He had placed his Peacemaker at the centre of the table. This was his way of letting his men know that he did not make idle threats. He did indeed expect every last one of them to be able to ride once the call came.

The big lawman was positioned at the bar. From time to

time the lawman glanced Epson's way. Epson ignored the lawman.

At the bar Sheriff John Sloan began to figure that Epson was waiting. But for what Sloan could not say. The atmosphere inside the saloon was uneasy.

'Hey, lawman, ain't you got nothing better to do than gawk?' an Epson man jeered.

Epson's fist hit the table. 'Button your lip, Patrick,' he snarled, and Patrick, with a glare at the lawman, turned away. Sloan ordered a second tepid beer. He was sipping the beer when a dust-covered galoot burst through the batwings.

'Hold-up,' he yelled. 'Hold up at the Frobisher mine. Those damn Coyotes have hit the Frobisher mine.'

'And Frobisher, he's dead?' the lawman demanded.

'Hell, he weren't even there. Boss Frobisher left the mine wide open.'

'Why?'

'Hell, I can't say. Say, are you gonna gab all day? Or are you gonna do something about it?' Garvey paused. He hated lawmen. 'Boss Frobisher reckons you ain't worth a spit,' he advised, grinning insolently.

Epson raised his Peacemaker. He fired two shots in rapid succession. It was the signal his men were waiting for. The signal that told them it was time to ride.

'Well it's lucky for your boss I'm here. You stay put, lawman. This is man's work.' He spat into the sawdust.

'Don't show your face in this town again,' Sheriff Sloan warned.

'You can count on that,' Epson rejoined as men tumbled down the stairs from the upstairs rooms, most of them in a state of partial dress.

'Let's ride,' Epson yelled. 'We've work to do. Frobisher's mine has been looted.'

'I need men to deputize,' Sloan yelled. 'And no, we ain't going after the Coyotes. The Frobisher mine is our first and last stop.' He had to do something. Folk in town had heard the carelessly uttered insult. 'Like the rest of folk hereabouts, Norman Frobisher ain't above the law although he may think he is. Well, it's time to put him and his investors straight. And any varmint who refuses to be deputized is in danger of losing his goddamn head. Am I making myself clear?'

Even as he spoke the lawman suddenly realized that Epson had been sitting waiting for news that the mine had been held up. It had to be so. The man had not been merely idling away time. His stay in Poynton had been absolutely necessary, for Epson could not ride out until the right moment arrived.

'Boss, boss,' White bellowed as Frobisher thundered through the gates of the mine.

The five scattered bodies told Frobisher all he needed to know. The gold was gone. He'd been lured out for the purpose of robbery.

'They ain't that far ahead!' White exclaimed excitedly. 'We can run them down.'

'Hell, boss, our horses are run into the ground,' Edwards remonstrated.

'Those damn Coyotes are loaded down with our gold. I don't reckon they can make good speed,' someone observed.

'Say, boss, is there a bonus in this for us?' another asked.

Frobisher forced his mouth into the semblance of a grin. He then clamped a cigar between his teeth. He lit the cigar and inhaled. Appearance was everything. He could not let his men see that he was running scared. And it wouldn't take long for his crew to figure out that he'd been a damn fool.

'There sure is.' He grinned. 'I want the ears of every last one of them. And we're gonna get those ears. And as for you, White,' he turned his head and smiled down at White.

'Yes boss.'

'When you signed up didn't you agree to protect my mine to your last breath?'

'I sure did, boss.' White did not see the trap.

'Well, I guess it's time you honoured your agreements. Your pards are waiting.' As White stared uncomprehendingly, Frobisher drew his Peacemaker and put a bullet through White's forehead. 'Those damn no-goods could have held this mine against the odds and that's a fact.' He pointed at an overturned table and scattered cards. The varmints had let him down.

'Ain't we best tote them inside and get them covered?' There was no response. 'Damn flies,' Edwards concluded when the boss ignored him.

'You stay behind, Edwards. When I get back I want to see they've been planted. Get digging,' Frobisher snarled, knowing the man's hands would blister mighty bad before the job was done, for the soil was rock solid.

Edwards nodded.

'OK, you men. Let's ride! We're gonna get back what is

ours. But we must take account of the fact that the horses have been run hard, so we ain't galloping out like the devil is at our heels. Slow but sure is the order of the day. And keep your eyes peeled for ambush. Those varmints will be expecting pursuit.'

No one spoke. Frobisher knew none of them had the stomach to challenge him.

'Hell, I sure hope we ain't called upon to wet-nurse these no-account drunkards more than a day or so,' Riley griped.

'Riley, you leave that jug of rotgut liquor be,' Yancey advised. 'You're here to work, not to indulge your liking for liquor.'

'Quit bellyaching.' Riley laughed.

'Well, I ain't wet-nursing you,' Yancey grumbled.

'And who asked you to!' Riley yelled, his good humour fading. His face reddened and he drew back a fist.

'Hell, I didn't mean to speak out of turn,' Yancey grovelled.

Riley smiled. His good humour had returned. 'I'll overlook it this one time,' he offered magnanimously.

Yancey turned away in disgust. Inside the line cabin the men had already found the liquor left by the boss. Yancey made a half-hearted attempt at warning the no-accounts to leave the liquor be but the temptation was too much and they ignored him, as he had known they would.

'Well, I aim to get myself fresh air,' Yancey observed. Wild horses would not get him inside the line cabin.

CHAPTER 10

Kent led his men along the dry gully. When this was over he and Lilly were headed for Europe, where they would live like royalty.

His men were euphoric, believing that soon they would be going their separate ways richer than they could ever have imagined. Kent had long ago realized that this could not be allowed to happen. Not one of them could be trusted not to ruin the set-up he had so carefully worked towards.

The Coyotes had to be believed to be dead. For this goal to be achieved they all had to lie low. He had always maintained rigid discipline. Every man had to be afraid to step out of line. He knew damn well that once his men were beyond his reach caution and discipline would soon be abandoned as they pursued a life given to drink, gambling and accommodating women.

'Without you they are nothing,' Lilly had told him.

He'd become smitten with Lilly. And he'd found he hadn't cared what had really brought her West. She'd proved herself as ruthless as he.

'Hell boss! You've done it. You've pulled it off.' Nash

howled like a coyote and the others followed suit.

'We've all done it,' Kent corrected. 'Hell, I'm sure going to miss you men.' And it was true. He would miss the old life. But, as Lilly said, a new and better life beckoned. He smiled and accepted their praise without the slightest twinge of conscience. Indeed it would be impossible to have a conscience considering the way he'd been raised.

Rounding a bend in the gully they spotted the peddler's wagon waiting just where arranged. Moonface, standing beside the wagon, waved his hat and gave a whoop as he spotted them.

'Glory be, here you are!' he yelled. 'Come on! Come on! I've work to do.'

'Get his team unhitched,' Kent ordered.

'Hell, the old varmint sure does stink,' Nash muttered.

Kent watched as the wagon team was unhitched. Moonface had become a stinking old varmint. When this last job was over the old man would no longer be an asset. He'd be a stone around the neck dragging a man down.

'Mind you leave me a horse well-tethered, boy,' Moonface snarled.

'Hell, who are you calling boy?' Nash challenged.

The peddler merely shrugged.

Get to it, boy. Moonface had snarled throughout Kent's childhood, often emphasizing the order with a well-placed kick. Yet the old fool believed he too was destined for Europe. Age must have addled his wits. Mighty soon the old goat would be getting his just deserts. As whatever conscience Kent might once have possessed had vanished long ago, this was not a problem.

'Trust me,' he reassured the disgusting old coot. 'I'll

tether your horse myself. It won't break free when the ruckus starts.'

'Hell, I know, boy. I know.' Moonface smiled fondly.

'Hell, how is this old coot going to deal with Frobisher?' Nash questioned.

'Stay around and find out,' the peddler offered.

Nash shook his head. There was something about the old man that made him afraid. It was a fool notion he knew but he could not shake it off.

'No. If the boss trusts you that's good enough.'

As they rode out Kent realized that he was the only one among them that had absolute faith in the old man. He smiled grimly; few knew just what the oldster was capable of.

Alone, Moonface prepared for the destruction of Frobisher. Hidden inside his wagon was his prize possession, kept in perfect working order over the years. He was looking forward to what was to come. He had always wanted to use the Gatling gun.

Needing room, he tossed out goods no longer needed. Washboards followed frying pans and kettles as he cleared out his wagon. His peddling days were over.

Frobisher kept his eyes peeled for any sign of a trap as they followed the gully, even though this place did not give itself to ambush for there no places of concealment. An ambush if it came would be when they left the gully.

'Hold up!' he yelled when, rounding a bend in the trail, they spotted the peddler's teamless wagon up ahead. Discarded goods were scattered around. There was no sign of movement.

They were stopped just beyond gunshot range. It seemed likely that now the old peddler was no damn use the Coyotes had left him dead in the wagon after unhitching the team. It was what Frobisher himself would have done.

He was damn sure the old coot was lying inside the wagon with his throat cut, but the wagon had to be checked out before they could move ahead.

'Aw, come on. It's safe enough,' Johnson, one of the men who'd seen off Joe Morgan, declared. 'I'll throw that old coot out for the buzzards.' Without waiting for Frobisher's say-so Johnson rode ahead.

No one fired. There was no sign of movement and Johnson, with a wave of his hat, disappeared into the wagon. Inside the stinking gloom of the wagon he made out a prone figure and something else as well.

Frobisher waited. There was nothing. And then Johnson called out. 'Old coot's dead but there's things in this wagon you ought to see.'

'What are we waiting for?' Brown spurred his horse. Truth was he had begun to lose respect for Frobisher. The boss had shown poor judgement.

'Goddamnit!' Frobisher bellowed angrily, now obliged to follow on in the rear instead of taking his rightful place in the lead.

Moonface calmly slit the cowardly mine guard's throat. How the hell the fool thought he'd be allowed to live for betraying his friends the peddler did not know.

'Thank the Lord,' he yelled as he fired the Gatling. Men and horses, screaming, went down like a house of cards. They did not stand a chance. 'Thank the Lord for fools,' the peddler screamed as he wreaked carnage.

Blood seemed to be spurting all around as Flobisher's horse went down. Mercifully he wasn't hit. He howled with pain for his leg was partly trapped beneath the animal. A figure ambled towards him. a long wickedly curved knife in hand.

The peddler grinned. 'I ain't never liked you, Boss Frobisher,' he cackled.

As Sheriff John Sloan was riding out of town the stage had just arrived. Sloan stopped to watch the passengers alight He stared at the large woman. She was respectably dressed but overloaded with rings.

'Direct me to where I can find Harriet Broughton!' She waved a hand at him as if he were of little consequence.

Curtly Sloan gave directions before riding out. He had no time for her right now.

Picking up her skirt Miz Clara headed for Miz Mattie's shack. Dire necessity had brought her West. Broughton's father's heart had given out. And now the cousin aimed to take that paper and use that paper to close down her establishment. This was common knowledge. It was too damn risky for her to arrange an accident so she'd thought of another way.

She detected an air of expectancy in the town and found herself wondering what the hell was going on in this no-account dump.

'You there,' she stopped a townsman by grabbing his arm. 'Is Rumble in town?'

The man shook his head. 'Nope, the doc has ridden out on a horse which ain't fit for nothing but stew or glue. Folk reckon he's gotten himself lost. He's a city gent after all.'

'Damnation!' she muttered, continuing on her way.

Yancey had roasted a goat over an open fire.

'Seems you men deserve a meal,' he observed dully as Kent and the crew appeared from amongst the trees. Fat dripped down his chin. He wiped it away with his bandanna.

Kent didn't give a damn about food. 'Yancey, are they all inside?'

'Every last one.' Yancey confirmed. 'Along with Riley. He's passed out with the rest of them.'

'We must leave him be then.' Kent shook his head. No one argued. It irked him to see that men were cutting themselves off hunks of roast meat. He'd not told them to eat. Already his authority was slipping.

'Ain't no way none of those bums can get out of the cabin.' Yancey laughed, noticing that Kent seemed ill-pleased.

'Hell, boss! If Epson don't find them what then?' a man essayed.

Kent glared at the speaker. 'I don't care for the word "if". As soon as Epson learns of the hold-up he'll be on his way.' Unexpectedly he smiled. 'Our guests, of course, will await upon the captain's arrival. They cannot get out!'

Epson rode into the Frobisher mine. 'Howdy there. I'm Captain Epson.'

The man left behind squinted at him. 'You ain't needed. The boss is taking care of this matter himself.'

Epson laughed. 'You damn fool! Frobisher ain't the

133

man to deal with the Coyotes. Ride along with us if you like and you'll discover the truth of the matter.'

Edwards hesitated. He shook his head. 'Frobisher would have my hide if I left this place unmanned. I'm obliged to keep an eye on the work force.'

'The slaves!'

'Hell, no. The Chinese are all free men.'

'Who ain't able to leave! But that ain't my business.' Epson shook his head. 'Your boss will find there ain't no one in this territory capable of dealing with those damn owl hoots save myself and my crew. We'll pick up the trail from here.'

As Edwards watched the men ride out he reflected that Epson was a conceited cuss. Epson and Frobisher had conceit in common, that was for sure, he decided. Settling down to wait he helped himself to one of Frobisher's fine cigars.

He was on his third cigar when the sound of riders announced he had company once again. He hefted his shotgun, knowing it was too damn soon for Frobisher to have retuned. To his disbelief he saw that Sheriff John Sloan had actually left Poynton.

'Hell, you ain't needed, Sheriff,' Edwards sneered. 'Captain Epson is in hot pursuit. Not that he'll be needed, for Mr Frobisher will take care of this matter himself. You've had a wasted journey.' When the lawman did not reply Edwards winked. 'I see your posse ain't up to much! Hell, you must have scraped the bottom of the barrel. Ain't that the barber and storekeep I see?' He spat. 'If it comes to a shootout you'll find them no darn use.'

'Well it won't come to that, for I see you are here solo.'

Sloan laughed. 'I'm not here to help your boss out of the hole he's dug for himself. I've turned a blind eye to the wrongdoing at this mine long enough. Get that shed unlocked, I'm removing your so-called workers to the safety of town. If Frobisher don't like it he can come to town. I'll put him straight.'

'You can't do that,' Edwards blustered.

'I'm the law in these parts. Get that shed unlocked lest I be tempted to put a slug through your fool head.'

'You're making a big mistake. It don't do to rile the boss,' Edwards threatened, remembering the unfortunate Doc Rumble!

'Don't argue with me, you polecat. Do as I say. This is your last chance. Frobisher ain't worth dying for, is he?'

Cussing beneath his breath, Edwards felt obliged to comply.

Sloan cussed as the miserable wretches kept prisoner by Frobisher emerged into the light of day.

In Miz Mattie's home the three women sat drinking tea.

'The fact is, now that your pa has passed over your scheming cousin intends to have you declared insane and take the paper.'

'So why should you care?' Miz Mattie asked bluntly.

'Once he's got the paper he'll use it to get me closed down,' Clara explained. 'Not on account of principles for he ain't got none. Fact is I had him thrown out of my establishment when he started haggling over the price.' She shook her head. 'It ain't wise for me to arrange an accident. But you'll owe me, Miss Broughton, for I have warned you. I expect you to leave my establishment be. I don't want to see a word in print.'

'I won't do it,' Harriet Broughton gasped. But she wasn't talking about Clara's establishment. 'Can't you think of anyone else?'

'You ain't never going to be able to go back East if you don't go along with my suggestion,' Miz Clara explained, 'Besides which Dennis Rumble ain't going to be interested in you or your paper. He owes me. And now I am calling in my debt. Ain't no way your cousin can do you harm if you have a husband and that husband happens to be called Rumble.'

There was a long uncomfortable silence.

'My father died in his carriage, you say?' Harriet Broughton muttered.

'Yep. Seems his heart just gave out.'

'But he didn't die in his carriage, did he? He died in your house of ill-repute and was put in his carriage!'

'You go around making those claims, Miss Broughton, and folk will know you have gone crazy. You smile and play the game like everyone else and if you don't want your cousin to have the paper you'll follow my advice.'

'But Rumble!'

'What happened to Judge Thompson?' Mattie interrupted. 'You seem a well-informed woman.'

'Well, so I am. But it's best you don't know. It was not my doing.' Miz Clara sipped her tea. 'Rumble asked me to help out an unfortunate soul named Miss Kathleen Clegg. Suffice it to say she dealt with Judge Thompson before she left these shores.'

Harriet Broughton nodded very slowly. 'But Rumble. . . ?'

'Owes me and knows damn well he has got to pay.' Miz Clara smiled. 'That's the way it is. He won't like it but I ain't giving him a choice. And if the varmint thinks he's going to stay around Poynton he's mistaken. As soon as he gets back we're headed out, Miss Broughton. Whatever reason brought him to Poynton ain't relevant now, for Judge Thompson . . . well, we won't be seeing him again.'

'What have we here?' Epson asked unnecessarily, for everyone could see a massacre had occurred. Carnage was strewn all around, dead men and horses already beset by swarms of buzzing black flies. And clearly the buzzards had started filling their gullets.

One of the men who had not ridden with Epson previously spewed up his last meal.

'Easy there.' Epson made a show of patting the weakling on the back. 'Like I explained when you signed up, we go after the worst kind of varmints. That's why we deal with them before they can deal with us. That's how come we've stayed alive so long.' He looked the man in the eye. 'I've a job for you. You're gonna head back to town and report what we have discovered. You are to say matters are in hand. Now mount up and get going.'

His man needed no further urging.

Epson watched the weakling ride out. He'd always made a habit of weeding them out. Not that he hired many, but occasionally one would slip through the net.

'Damn varmints,' his men muttered.

But whether they were referring to the murdered mine owner and his employees or the nefarious Coyotes was hard to say.

If ever Epson needed proof that his grandfather was a mad old cuss this was it. The old man had gone loco, plunging his blade time and time again into the faces of the men he had killed.

'Leastways, we know the kind of scum we are after,' he observed loudly. 'But we knew that before. When we hunt this particular bunch down I ain't disposed to show them mercy.'

Loud hoots of approval greeted his assertion.

'Well, we must leave them as they fell,' he continued. 'No-accounts such as that lawman can see to the burying of them. Sloan ain't much use for anything else and that's a fact.' He swung into the saddle. 'Let's ride.' He'd make a pretence of following the tracks but he knew damn well where that they were headed for Richard's line cabin. This particular plan had been worked out way back between himself, his brother who now called himself Richard Kent, and the old cuss who was their grandfather.

Epson spat. He hated his relatives. Too bad they would not be inside the line cabin!

Riley groaned. His skull felt on fire. As the room span around him he levered himself into a sitting position.

The air inside the cabin was fetid and clogged with the stink of rotgut liquor. He managed to get to his feet and, heedless of the prone bodies strewn around, made his way to the door, for he urgently needed to relieve himself.

'Goddamnit,' he bellowed as the door refused to budge. Continuing to yell profanities he hammered and kicked at the door.

'Yancey, you polecat, I need out! Where the hell are

you? Get me out of here.'

Through the narrow window slit he saw that dawn had broken. Within the cabin, roused by the noise, men were scratching and profaning and beginning to stir. Riley's heart began to thud uncomfortably, for there was no sign of Yancey!

'You damn varmints,' a voice yelled from a spot out of the view from the window. 'I'm Captain Epson. You put the stolen gold out through the window real slow and I vow you'll all get a fair trial.'

'Hell, mister, we ain't no thieves,' a bum gabbled as he shoved Riley out of his way. 'We ain't got no damn gold and that's a fact.'

'One last chance!' Epson played to his crew.

'Open this goddamn door,' Riley bellowed. 'We can talk. We ain't those damn Coyotes, just hard-working waddies in the employ of Boss Kent, owner of the Lazy R Ranch.'

'Who we've tracked right to this very cabin,' Epson rejoined. 'I want that gold. What do you say? Will you bargain to save your hides?'

'You go to hell, you varmint.' A bum discharged a shotgun through the window.

Riley sniffed. Something sure smelt strange. And then with horror he realized what was about to happen.

'You Coyotes ain't dealing with Frobisher now!' Epson raised his hand and the men he had already placed in position around the cabin fired the kerosene-soaked hay they had piled high around the place.

'For mercy's sake,' Riley screamed. 'We've been set up, do you hear?' But no one heard him for inside the cabin pandemonium had broken out as terrified men screamed and bellowed.

Epson watched dispassionately as the fire took hold. The screams from inside the inferno did not move him.

'What about Frobisher's gold?' a man asked.

'The varmints have hidden it away,' Epson declared. 'We'll retrace our footsteps keeping a sharp eye out for hidey-holes. Maybe we'll strike lucky. Maybe not! Whatever we find is ours.'

He almost laughed at the faces of the fools he was riding with, for they believed every word, all of them believing they would strike lucky and find the gold.

The cabin door was aflame now and a man resembling a flaming torch stumbled out and staggered crazily before keeling over.

Epson watched dispassionately, thinking old Moonface would have hooted with laughter at such a sight.

No one else made it out of the burning cabin. Thick black smoke spiralled skyward.

'Come on, boss,' a man urged as Epson rolled a smoke. 'Let's root out the gold!'

'Hell, boss,' one of them grumbled. 'This way we can't question the varmints. We could have made 'em talk if only we'd grabbed a couple alive.'

'Maybe so,' Epson wisely agreed. 'But the cards did not fall that way. But you're right. My smoke can wait.' He must let them ride themselves ragged searching for gold and then, when they'd run out of steam he'd finally get them back to Poynton. He'd pay them off and they would disband. Not coming together until another job came their way. Or so they would believe. Epson knew he'd seen the back of them. This had been the last hunting party he would ever lead.

Higgins burst in the jailhouse. 'Epson's back,' he announced.

Sloan picked up his shotgun. Slowly he made his way down Main Street towards the livery barn. He aimed to see that Epson and his men did not stay around Poynton longer than they needed. He'd decided to leave Frobisher for the buzzards or for the men the company back East was bound to send out to replace those lost.

'It's over with, Sheriff. The Coyotes won't be troubling this territory again. As I suspected Richard Kent, boss of the Lazy R, and his crew were the Coyotes. They've been dealt with.' Epson waved a hand. 'You men head over to the hotel. I'll join you shortly.' And so he would, to pay them off.

'And the gold?'

'We ain't seen a sign of it Do my men look as if they have gold in their pockets?'

'So where are the bodies?' the lawman asked drily, deciding not to pursue the matter of the missing gold, for the glum faces of Epson's men spoke louder than any words.

'There's nothing left of them to tote back to town.' Epson winked. 'Fact is I was obliged to burn them out. You've heard what befell Frobisher?'

'Yep. Your man reported as ordered.'

'You'll see to them?'

Sloan shook his head.

'Well, it ain't my concern. But they'll be sending out

investigators from back East to scour the territory and to determine just what has been going on hereabouts.'

'I want you out of my town,' the lawman stated bluntly, 'for the stink of death hangs over you, Epson.'

'I understand. I've dealt with those damn Coyotes. I've done your job for you, Sloan. I've no mind to stay around your two-bit town. I'll pay off the men and ride out. I know damn well how you are feeling. You've been found wanting and you know it.'

'Pay off your men and then shake the dust of my town from your boots.'

'Say, Captain Epson, have you seen Doc Rumble?' Higgins, who had joined the pair, spoke up.

'I reckon he's dead,' Epson drawled. 'I never figured Rumble was the man folk figured him to be. He's a no-account sewage rat at home amongst the garbage. He ought not to have travelled West. Certainly if he was hired to deal with the Coyotes he ain't earned his money. Hell, sending Rumble West to deal with the Coyotes was one hell of a joke. If anyone had asked I could have told them so.' He shrugged. 'It's lucky for the varmint I did not see him, for I would have been tempted to deal with him. Now, if you gentlemen will excuse me I have matters needing my attenetion.'

'You look worried, Higgins,' Sloan observed.

'If I could get word to the doc I'd warn him, that's for sure.' Higgins shifted uncomfortably. 'Fact is, the cards ain't falling in his favour, for those women are conspiring against him. Word is he is obliged to get hitched to Miss Harriet Broughton.'

'What?'

'Well, more than that I cannot say.' Higgins began to turn away. 'Do you think the doc can make it back to town?'

Sloan shrugged. 'I'm damned if I know! But either way it looks as if his luck has run out.'

CHAPTER 11

Rumble knew that it was time to come down from the fence. He had to do what he'd come West to do, rescue Miss Lillian Thompson and wipe out the Coyotes.

He decided to head first of all for Frobisher's mine. He needed supplies. Of late he'd been reduced to eating hard biscuit soaked in tepid water. He was willing to gamble he would not find Frobisher at home. The Coyotes would have seen to it that Frobisher and crew had been wiped out.

He put the old bloodstained journal in his back pocket. He believed he knew where he would be able to find the Coyotes. But before he could set about finding them he must get down from this damn mountain. And hell, that was going to take some time! He would not risk slipping and breaking a leg or maybe even his head. Yep, that would be best. If he were destined to break anything a head would be preferable to a leg. Leastways his exit would be quick!

And when he did get down he'd have to encourage his horse to get moving for it was inclined to want to stay put.

But leastways, with the help of the journal and a compass it would be damn hard to become lost.

Kent led his men along the narrow twisting trail climbing higher and higher into the hills. He was looking forward to seeing Lilly again. He guessed by now she would have chewed her nails down to nothing as she waited upon his return. She had her own part to play in all of this and she knew better than to let him down.

Overhanging branches whipped into the faces of the Coyotes as they headed for their final destination. Kent never would have known about this particular hideout had his grandpa not taken a dead man's journal.

Old memories, long buried, surfaced. That English gentleman had been a long time dying. Grandpa had seen to that.

Stunted bushes gave way to cold grey slabs of rock. Ahead was the narrow mouth of the concealed cave where the men expected to lie low before heading out, each one with his share of the loot.

Kent paused to wipe his brow. 'We'll lead the horses from here on,' he ordered, for the ground was treacherous.

'Say, Yancey, why'd you let your pard Riley bed down with those goddamn bums?' a Coyote reproached.

'Men like us,' Yancey answered. 'well, we don't have pards. We can't afford to have them. Ain't that so, boss?'

Kent did not trouble to reply to the fool question, although Yancey had never spoken a truer word. 'Well, we've all made it!' He pointed to the mouth of the cave. 'And unless I am mistaken Miss Lilly is busy right now cooking up something mighty special. Hell, I could do with a decent meal. I reckon we've earned it. What do you say?'

'Miss Lilly is here?' Yancey questioned.

'Well, she sure is. I'm not going anywhere without that little lady,' Kent joshed. 'She's an amazing woman.' And she sure was; when it had came to ridding himself of these fools she'd known just the way to do it. From the time he'd removed her from the stage after killing the driver and the other passengers she'd never ceased to amaze him. Her ingenuity matched his own.

'We can poison the lot of them,' she had said. 'Just you make sure every last one of them takes a plate of my stew.'

Inside the cave Miss Lilly stirred the pot. It smelt good. Daydreaming about the gold she'd almost made the mistake of tasting a spoonful of the special stew. Just in time she'd stopped herself. Soon it would all be over with.

When she'd fled West to find her son, the baby Kathleen Clegg had left on the orphanage porch, she hadn't known what she was doing. Now she didn't want the child. He'd only be a hindrance, she had come to believe.

With the money and gold Richard Kent had stolen they'd both be able to live like royalty. She had big plans. They would assume new identities and travel to Europe. And when they reached Europe Richard Kent could meet with an accident. She was as yet undecided about the matter.

The sound of hoofs on shale let her know the men were here. With an effort she assumed a welcoming smile. She knew damn well that it was only Kent's protection that had stopped the crew from falling on her like the rabid dogs they were. If anyone deserved a dose of poison it was them! And she was more than happy to oblige.

There was enough room in the cave for the horses. She hoped the stink of the horses wouldn't stop the crew from enjoying her stew. But no! Some of them stank worse than the horses.

'Hey there, Lilly, I've some hungry men in need of feeding,' Kent shouted jovially.

'And my stew is mighty fine if I do say so myself,' she yelled back. 'It's ready and waiting.' She began to ladle out bowls. She made damn sure there was a bowl for each of them.

'Well, Riley won't be needing his victuals.' One of them actually helped himself to a double portion.

'Eat up and then we will divide the plunder,' Kent encouraged.

Upon hearing this the men began shovelling down the stew as if they were shovelling coal into an engine.

'Ain't you eating, boss?' Yancey asked.

'Later. Me and Lilly have matters to attend to.' To loud hoots of encouragement he hauled Lilly from the cave. But neither of them was in the mood for hanky-panky. In case things did not go to plan he drew his Peacemaker.

Lilly smiled reassuringly. 'It won't be long, Richard. It's quick-working.'

'Damnation, I'll miss them,' Kent stated. 'But it's got to be done. There ain't one of them who can be trusted not to mess up and get himself arrested and identified as a Coyote.'

'But the waiting is hard. I understand.' Lilly stroked his arm.

'You're damn right it is!'

Inside the cave a man doubled over clutching his stomach. Others began to follow.

A terrible griping pain gripped Yancey. He drew his shooter and staggered towards the cave entrance. Another wave hit him. He could hardly see. As he staggered into the open he fired at the two blurred figures. As he fell his last thought was that his slug had gone wide.

A man came crawling out of the cave. This time, taking no chances, Kent put a slug in the man's head.

And then they waited for it all to be over.

'Damnation. I'll never touch another plate of stew.' Kent tried to joke.

'And I'll never cook another pot of stew,' Lilly replied. 'We'll have servants of course. We'll be the talk of the town with our entertaining.'

'Yancey was a fighter to the last,' Kent observed when the noise made by the dying had ceased. 'Leastways he went out still fighting.' His smile faded. 'And now,' he continued, 'we must wait for the old man and Captain Epson. Sure as hell I have a surprise in store for that old coot'

'Be careful,' Lilly whispered. 'There's something about that old man that makes my blood run cold.'

'You can't tell me anything about that old coot I don't already know,' Kent rejoined. 'We'll tie up the loose ends, two of them to be precise, and then we'll fork it out pretty damn quick.'

Against his better judgement Edwards, instead of heading for town, had ridden out to where Frobisher had met his end. One of Epson's men having swung by the mine had told him what had occurred.

'Damn varmints!' Edward declared. Clearly no one hereabouts could be troubled to at least do the decent thing and retrieve the remains. Buzzards had flapped away at Edward's approach but now, as he stood indecisively, they grew bold and waddled in to resume the feast.

His stomach churned. The only man who could have ambushed and killed this bunch was Moonface. The Gatling, now rendered useless, lay beside the wagon. Edwards could easily imagine the barrage of bullets tearing into flesh. Horses and men had gone. Those animals not killed outright had been dispatched with a bullet. Men had not been so lucky. The old man had gone crazy hacking away with his knife and as for Frobisher, well, his end had been hard.

Stomach still churning he left this scene of carnage and headed for the line cabin where the Coyotes had been burnt alive by Epson. With his boot he began to unearth all that remained of the outlaws: just blackened bones. That the Coyotes who had hitherto prospered had been so foolish as to be caught napping by Epson did not sound right. Those galoots would not have drunk themselves into a stupor. Lookouts would have been posted. And why hole up in this cabin? He didn't know. He didn't give a damn now about anything other than the gold. It was out there somewhere for the taking, if a man knew where to look.

And damnation, he was going to look. If there were a trail to be found he would find it. And why the hell if there was such a trail hadn't Epson followed on? Why had he headed straight back to town once the killing was over? Sure as hell the investigators who would be swarming over the territory would be asking plenty of questions.

He was damned afraid. But this was his chance. He was going to follow the trail up into the hills. He was going after the devil's gold.

Captain Epson rode out of Poynton just as trouble was breaking out in the saloon.

Sheriff John Sloan, headed for the saloon with his shotgun beneath his arm, hardly spared Epson a glance. He knew damn well that Epson's hirelings were getting themselves as drunk as skunks.

'Say there, Captain Epson, if you meet that no-account varmint Doc Rumble put a slug in him,' a man bellowed, staggering out from an alleyway. Epson spurred his horse forward and Casper narrowly avoided being run down.

Epson rode on without looking back. Mighty soon he would be meeting up with his brother, the man calling himself Richard Kent, and their grandfather, the peddler known as Moonface.

Grandpa would not be coming down from the cave. Epson also contemplated disposing of his brother. It was the best way. And no doubt his brother would be having similar thoughts.

Perspiration dripped down Kent's face. He'd been working damn hard. He'd set a trap across the trail leading upwards. The trap had been set at the narrowest point. It was intended for Moonface, who should have shown up by now. But then the old coot had always been unpredictable. And if his brother should be the first to arrive, well, that was too bad.

Moonface had taken a detour. He'd swung by his grandson's ranch in the hope that the fine woman Richard was keeping had been left under lock and key; that was if she was still alive. He still fancied the ladies. Trouble was they didn't fancy him.

'Goddamnit,' he cussed when he found no sign of the woman either alive or dead; he felt as if he'd been cheated out of his fun. She could only be with his grandson in the cave. Which meant that the fool cared more for the woman than was wise. Well, he could always spruce himself up when he got the gold. Women would want him then. Cussing his grandson he rode to keep the rendezvous.

Kent heard the rider on the trail. He wouldn't be able to identify the rider before he sprang the trap. The stench that normally accompanied Grandpa was absent so he guessed the man was his brother. For a moment he hesitated, unsure what to do, but hell, his brother would have no qualms about getting rid of him.

As the rider drew level Kent cut the rope holding back the branch. It sprang forward, the spiked wire carefully wrapped around it thudding into the man's throat, the momentum of the movement thrusting the barbs deeply into the skin.

As horse and man went down Kent emerged from his hiding-place. He shot the threshing horse then cussed when he saw that the man choking upon his own blood was neither of the two he needed to be rid of. He recognized the galoot as belonging to the Frobisher mine.

Heading for the cave Epson passed a body lying on the trail. There was also the butchered remains of a horse. He thinned his lips. It could have been him. He reckoned it was his brother who had set the trap. He did not think the old man would have done it. When he reached the cave he found his grandpa drying strips of meat over a low fire.

'Seems like your brother tried to kill me!' Moonface cackled. He did not sound displeased.

'Now, Grandpa, I know you would not be fool enough to ride into a trap.' Kent laughed. 'But, like you say, a man can never be too careful.' He waited for Epson to say something.

Epson masked his anger as he greeted the woman he guessed to be Miss Lillian Thompson. Rumour had it she'd run off although the judge had always vehemently denied the rumour.

'It seems your pa has upped and disappeared. If anyone knows his whereabouts they ain't saying!'

Miss Lillian merely shrugged. And then she frowned. 'But what of Rumble?'

Epson laughed, 'I haven't discovered what hold your pa had over him, how it was he got Rumble headed West to rescue you, Miss Lilly, but the judge sure as hell misjudged his man, for Rumble's always been a no-account varmint.' Epson spat to signify his opinion of Dennis Rumble. 'I guess we don't need to worry about the doc,' he concluded scornfully.

'Hell, he treated me!' Moonface cackled. 'The man's a mighty fine doc. And, he never looked to be a damn fool.

He seemed a capable kind of galoot!'

'Hell, that crazy old woman Mattie proved more of a threat than the doc.'

'Yep. I heard about her.'

'Lucky for us she ain't on our trail,' Moonface joshed. 'But I still ain't convinced about the doc!'

'Word in town is that he's dead. He ain't got the skills to survive. He doesn't know the territory and the horse he took is no damn use.' Epson turned his attention to Miss Lilly. 'I reckon I know why you headed West, Miss Lilly!' he taunted.

'And why is that?' Kent demanded softly.

Epson laughed. 'Why, in search of adventure of course. And you sure have found it.'

'Along with the gold.' Moonface didn't give a damn why Lillian Thompson had headed West. 'I say we keep our wits about us until we are clear of the territory. I don't want to see you boys at each other's throats. Do you hear me now? We ain't sure as yet that Rumble don't pose a threat.' His voice hardened the way it used to do when they were youngsters in need of learning.

The two men looked at one another. They didn't need to speak. The old man's days were numbered. For now they would work together, leastways until they had taken care of the crazy old varmint and got safely out of the territory.

Lillian Thompson awoke some time during the night. She lay for a moment listening to the breathing of her companions. The old man snored, loud disgusting noises that she found hard to stomach. And he smelt, not that it was possible to separate his smell from that of the rotting flesh of the dead men; covered with rocks, it was true, but only because she had made it clear to Richard Kent that a lady should not have to look at such a sight.

Needing to relieve herself, she silently left the cave. As she emerged into the open, a hand clamped over her mouth and she was pulled away from the cave entrance. She knew who it was before he spoke. Now when it was all over he'd turned up.

'Don't be afraid, Miss Lillian. I'm Dennis Rumble, hired by your pa to get you away from these no-account varmints.' There was a pause. 'And the fact is, Miss Lilly, you are due to come into an inheritance on your thirtieth birthday. The judge needs to produce you alive and well to get that money. But there ain't no way I'm taking you back unless you want to go. Trust me!' he whispered as he continued to draw her away from the cave. 'I'm gonna release you now. Just stay quiet. Leave the rest to me.'

The only thought in her mind was that Rumble had to be dealt with. Oh yes, she could go home and claim that miserly inheritance! But she could not allow Rumble to kill the men inside the cave, for Kent had hidden the gold. And he had not told her where. Nor had he told the other two.

'I ain't having the varmints turning on me,' he had said. 'We'll collect the loot when we ride out, and as for you, Miss Lilly, I ain't forgotten about your special stew.'

There was no way she could give up gold. No doubt she could have Rumble eating out of her hand but that would be no damn use without the gold.

Rumble took his hand away from her mouth and released her. He was prepared for her to collapse with fear.

He was ready to catch her should she faint. He was not prepared for what actually happened, Miss Lillian Thompson lunged at him, nails raking his face as she hysterically screamed his name.

Her hands grabbed at him. Long nails raked his face, missing an eye. And then as he tried to get free she tried to thrust a finger into his eye and she tried to bite him.

He was done for if he couldn't get away from her. The men inside were waking up.

'Quit struggling, Miss Lilly, or I'm done for.' His voice was rough. He was damn worried.

'You damn fool! Rot in hell,' she screeched.

It was then that Dennis Rumble knew he'd taken enough. Miss Lillian wanted him dead. She had truly thrown her lot in with Kent.

Kent, Epson and Moonface rushed to the mouth of the cave. Outside all was silence. Lilly's scream had stopped.

'Hold up. I reckon the varmint has a shotgun and aims to blast at any sign of movement. We're shooting blind. We don't want to die now we're rich men,' Moonface cackled. 'The woman ain't worth it.'

'We'll hunt him down at daybreak!' Epson decided. 'He won't get far with a woman slowing him down. For now we keep watch and stay awake in case the varmint tries something.'

'But Lilly—' Kent protested.

'We ain't no use to her dead.' Epson wasn't getting blasted rescuing his brother's woman.

'I'm gonna boil you real slow over a low fire,' Moonface yelled into the darkness. 'You're gonna suffer, Doc. You're gonna suffer!'

Mighty soon his boys were going to start questioning how Rumble had found them. He remembered that damn journal, filled with its fancy drawings and the cramped writing he could not read. For the first time in a long life he'd made one hell of a mistake.

'Hell, Doc,' he'd said, 'I ain't got the means to pay you in cash. While away your time with this,' he'd sneered. And Rumble, with a shrug, had accepted the dog-eared dirt-begrimed book.

'Say, Grandpa, what the hell happened to that old journal?' Richard had already began to figure things out.

'Hell, boy. How would I know? I lost it way back.'

'You ain't gone loco and given the doc that damn journal?'

'You're talking nonsense, boy,' Moonface snarled. 'Shut your mouth. You're riling me plenty. You two boys grab some shut-eye. I'll keep watch.' He positioned himself at the cave mouth, squatting cross-legged, rifle across his knees. To his relief, the boys quit gabbing.

The sound of the shot brought Epson awake, his hand reaching frantically for his Peacemaker.

The old man was sprawled face downwards by the cave entrance. It was clear he'd been backshot.

'He deserved it,' Kent declared. 'Hell, the old fool actually gave the doc that old journal. How else could he have found this place?'

'I reckon.' Epson stared at the body. His brother, who had hidden the gold, was calling the shots.

'We kill Rumble real slow. And then we'll divide the gold. Me and Lilly will head in one direction. You in another!'

Epson nodded. 'Let's run that varmint down!'

Leading their horses they left the safety of the cave. There was nowhere out on the flat grey rock for Rumble to hide. He'd be heading back down, hoping to outrun them, trying to find a spot to spring an ambush.

When Kent saw the body he gave a howl of pain. The polecat had killed Lilly. He stumbled to her and, kneeling beside her, saw that her neck had been snapped.

'Let's get moving. You can't help her.' Epson moved towards his brother.

Rumble, who was lying on the shallow shelf above the cave entrance, fired two shots in rapid succession. Kent's head exploded first. Epson's was a close second. He had no qualms about backshooting the pair. He'd known better than to run for his life. Hell, with his horse he would not stand a chance. He hadn't intended to kill Lilly but she'd fought him like a crazy woman.

It was over. He'd failed to rescue Lillian Thompson. The cards had fallen in ways he could not have anticipated.

He'd check out the cave for the damn gold but did not expect to find it. The Englishman had listed plenty of hiding-places he'd discovered during his exploration of the territory, and Kent as a boy would have seen the journal.

Too much blood had been spilt on account of the gold. It was the devil's gold. And, leastways for now, he wanted no part of it. He was a patient man, he could wait until the ruckus had died down, until those big-shot partners of Frobisher had accepted they'd never find the ill-gotten gold.

'Hell, we'd given up on you. All hell has been going on whilst you've been riding round in circles on that bag of bones.' Sheriff Sloan greeted him without enthusiasm as he rode into town. 'I'd keep riding if you don't want to find yourself hitched to Harriet Broughton.' And then Sloan grinned. 'Your luck has run out, Rumble. That no-account woman has seen you.'

Rumble had already spotted Miz Clara headed his way. And he knew she was behind whatever was afoot. He owed her and now she was calling in the debt.

She winked. 'There ain't no reason why you can't head back East. Judge Thompson has vanished without trace.' Disregarding the lawman she began to explain about Harriet Broughton, the cousin and the paper.

Rumble dismounted. He began to lead his horse towards the livery barn. He was trapped. He did owe her! But never had he imagined she would hatch up such a plan.

'Miss Broughton won't agree.' He tried to keep the hope from his voice.

'But she has.' Miz Clara smiled. 'And Miss Broughton, well, she wants to make peace with you. As a gesture of goodwill she'll pretend you are a true gentleman. And she says there's room in her stables for your riding horse. Higgins told her you were mighty taken with that particular horse.'

Harriet Broughton was clearly desperate.

'I don't want the paper or Miss Harriet Broughton.'

'Well, she doesn't want you. But you're the only man we

can trust. You'll do right. And it ain't got to be forever.'

'That's what you said when you visited me in the penetentiary. I survived that place. I can survive marriage with Harriet Broughton.'

The cards had not fallen as he would have wished but he'd still play them as best he could.